"Abby, about that proposal."

"I'm not going to talk about it, Donovan. It's over. I'm over it. I've moved on. So should you."

"You sound so hard. I don't remember that about you."

She stared straight at him.

"Time and circumstances do that to you, Donovan."

He returned her look without flinching.

"Maybe you should tell me what you think happened that night, Abby," he said, a quiet tension threading his voice. "What did your mother say?"

"What's the point in rehashing that period of our lives? It's over. Now, if you'll excuse me, I need to get back to work." Abby turned her back, pretending to concentrate on the ring in front of her.

A few minutes later, she heard the door close.

So Donovan was back.

So you avoid him, she thought. *Keep yourself busy and away from him. Donovan never sticks to anything anyway.* At least not the Donovan she remembered.

LOIS RICHER

A Ring and a Promise
Lois Richer

Steeple
Hill®

Published by Steeple Hill Books™

STEEPLE HILL BOOKS

Steeple
Hill®

Recycling programs
for this product may
not exist in your area.

ISBN-13: 978-0-373-87533-7

A RING AND A PROMISE

Copyright © 2009 by Lois M. Richer

www.SteepleHill.com

Printed in U.S.A.

Don't copy the behavior and customs of this world,
but be a new and different person with a freshness
in all you do and think.
—*Romans* 12:2

This book is for Lesley.

Chapter One

Doing your best usually meant redoing. Abigail Franklin had learned that at her mother's knee.

With a sigh, Abby squeezed her forceps, lifted the paste stone and dropped it in the center of her newest platinum setting for the third time.

"Looks good," a voice offered.

"Good is never good enough," she muttered. Then the familiar voice hit a nerve.

Abby's fingers numbed. Her forceps slid out of her hand. She lifted her head and stared.

"Hello, Abby."

He was back—after five long years.

Forcing taut muscles to obey, Abby slid from her stool and faced Donovan Woodward, the man who'd promised her the world. And never delivered.

Memories of that smile, all sparkle, charm and appeal, swamped her.

"I'm not an April Fool's joke, so stop staring," he ordered, his grin slashing his handsome face. "How are you?"

"Okay." She studied his jutting cheekbones. "And you?"

"I'm all right."

He didn't look all right. He looked tired.

But the longer Abby stared at Donovan Woodward, the more she knew tiredness wasn't the right word. True, there were deeply carved lines around his ocean-blue eyes, stripped now of the sparkle of pure fun that once dared her to join in. But tiredness wasn't the reason. Donovan never got tired, not the life-of-the-party Donovan that Abby had known.

Still, a girl didn't forget the face of the first man to ask her to marry him, even after five years. Yet his face had changed, matured.

"Aren't you going to say anything?" he demanded when the silence stretched too long and the air bristled with tenseness.

His testy tone irked her.

"Such as what? Welcome home?" Abby suggested, glaring at him. "Or maybe we could discuss that note you told my mother to give me five years ago. How did it go? 'I made a mistake. I'm leaving. Sorry.'"

She gritted her teeth, irked she'd let that slip out.

"That wasn't my best moment," he admitted. "But if you'll listen a minute, I'll explain—"

"After five years you're finally offering an explanation?" She tossed him a scathing glance before turning back to her work-table. "Forget it."

"Abby." Donovan touched her arm, wordlessly asking her to face him. "I know I should have explained my reasons to you personally. Asking you to marry me on prom night and leaving two days later for Europe wasn't exactly what I'd planned, but I figured you'd understand I was doing it for you."

"For me?" Incredulity filled her. "Is that how you justify it?"

"I didn't have to justify myself after—" Donovan shook his head, cleared his throat. "The gossip must have been awful. I'm sorry I left you alone to face that, Abby."

An apology from Donovan? That was nice. But all he was apologizing for was the gossip. He'd even intimated his leaving had somehow benefited her, which was ludicrous. But then, maybe five years in Europe had changed his memories.

Still, how could he say his decision had anything to do with her?

"The past is over, Donovan. Let's agree to disagree on your part in it." She refocused away from the painful memories. "Will you be working at Weddings by Woodwards?"

"Uh-huh." His shaggy walnut-toned hair moved in a ripple of assent.

"Your grandmother will be ecstatic. That's great." She winced as her voice echoed around her work room like some kind of cheerleader.

"Oh, Abigail. The way you say that," Donovan mocked.

"When did you get back?" Funny how she struggled to talk to him when once they'd never had enough time to say everything.

"Flew in tonight. Grandmother didn't tell me you'd be here," he mumbled with a frown at the array of tools she'd spread out.

"Sorry." If she'd known he was coming she'd have stayed away.

"Don't be. I needed to apologize, Abby. I owed you that."

"I don't want your apology."

"Tough. I needed to give it." A smile flirted with his lips, but didn't quite reach his eyes. "Want to reciprocate?"

"I have nothing to apologize for." Something lurked beneath the surface of his remarks, something Abby didn't understand. "Anyway, I told you, I don't want to discuss the past. We're different people now. I've moved on, Don. So have you, I'm sure."

He'd always been Don to her; charismatic, showering everyone in his life with laughter and happiness, always fun, totally irresistible.

And then he'd left.

"I'm sure you agree that leaving was the right thing to do, but I should have talked to you first. My only excuse is I was upset."

The right thing to do?

"Upset by what?" Confusion filled her. "Proposing?"

"No." He studied her intently. "Have you forgotten everything about that night, Abby?"

"I've tried," she said, meeting his stare. "It wasn't the best time of my life."

"Nor mine." Something lay hidden in those words. Something Donovan evidently decided not to clarify because after a moment of further scrutiny, he shrugged, stepped closer and brushed the edge of her creation with one fingertip. "Is this a special order?"

"A private commission." She studied the setting with a critical eye. Not her best yet, but better. "It's an idea for a project, actually."

Donovan nodded as if he'd expected that answer.

"What's the project?"

Abby didn't want to share her dream with him. But this awkwardness between them had to end. Weddings by Woodwards was a tight-knit family company that offered everything a bride and groom could need. Winifred Woodward expected her employees to get along.

"Is it a secret?"

"No." Abby strove for a bland tone, ignoring her inner discomfort. "It's for a contest in New York. Jewelry designers can submit fine designs. Well known designers will judge. It's great exposure and a chance to get my designs into New York. Entries close in two weeks." She bit her lip, then admitted the rest. "I haven't yet settled on the complete design."

"As I remember, you always had plans to go to New York."

With him. She'd thought they'd shared that dream.

"So what's holding you back?" Donovan leaned one hip against the counter and waited for her explanation.

"Time. My parents recently moved from their home into a retirement condo. It was a difficult transition."

"Ah, your parents."

Abby winced at his tone. Her mother had never accepted Donovan in her life. She'd always claimed he was never serious enough about anything. He'd endured her disapproval and caustic comments many times, and always without losing his charm. His faultless manners and quirky sense of humor had helped Abby weather many embarrassing confrontations.

"How are your parents? I suppose the two dedicated doctors of genetics are still buried in their world?"

"No. Dad's in the first stages of Alzheimer's. He gets frustrated by the memory lapses. Mom's finding it difficult." Wasn't that an understatement?

Her parents had always lived and breathed their work. They'd assumed Abby would follow in their footsteps and were less than pleased when she refused to attend college. Jewelry design was so *not* the career of choice her mother wanted for her only child, a fact she constantly reiterated.

"I'm very sorry, Abby." Donovan looked genuinely upset. "It can't be easy on you."

"I manage."

The casual hand he brushed through his hair, mussing it even further, was so Donovan. Abby blinked at the flicker of silver on his finger. He still wore the ring she'd made for him in junior high? That shocked her.

"So you entered this contest because—?"

Again Abby shoved back past memories.

"Because it's a once-in-a-lifetime opportunity to showcase my work to some of the top people in the industry. If I win, I'll finally be able to move to New York and work with one of them."

Donovan studied her solemnly.

"Still proving yourself, Abby?" he asked quietly.

She gripped the edge of her worktable and swallowed hard, suddenly furious.

"That's not fair. Don't I have a right to extend myself, see how far my abilities can take me? You're not the only one who has dreams beyond Denver you know."

Donovan's face altered. "I didn't mean that. You're a talented designer who can work marvels with metal and stone. It's only natural you want to stretch yourself."

"I can hear a 'but' in there."

He searched her face. The sparkle that usually blazed through his eyes dimmed.

"I know how hard you must have fought to make your own way, Abby."

"Nothing's changed there," she admitted grimly. "My mother still hopes I'll have some kind of awakening and realize I really want to be a scientist."

"Is she why you've entered this contest?"

The astuteness of his comment proved that Donovan had lost none of the perspicacity that had always rendered him capable of sizing up a situation in seconds. But Abby didn't want him looking too closely into her motives.

"I'm doing this for me," she told him firmly. "Because I need to stretch myself, to do more unusual designs, ones Weddings by Woodwards has no market for."

"And if winning means your mother finally accepts your capability, so much the better, right?" He nodded as if he understood. "I suppose it's the only way she'll be convinced now."

A simple uplift of one eyebrow breathed life into his entire face. Abby slammed the door on her memories. The past was dead. Her goal was the future.

"Have you got a stone chosen for this piece? You're surely not doing paste?"

"The fellow who commissioned it is buying the diamond from Woodwards."

"So you're looking at what, three carats?" he guessed. "Nice." He tilted his head to one side.

Then Donovan pulled a dark blue box from his jacket pocket.

"I saw this in Greece. It reminded me of that essay we did together in our senior year, the one on classical Greece."

She didn't want to talk about their past.

Donovan snapped the latch exposing a gorgeous bracelet crafted in the Byzantine style.

Abby lost her breath when he slid the web of gold onto her wrist. No sooner had he closed the clasp than she brought the bracelet closer to study it.

"The detail of the granulation is incredible. It looks like it was spun into shape." She twisted her arm left, then right, to examine each bend and fold, admiring the painstaking craftsmanship.

Then reality returned.

"I can't take this, Donovan. It's too expensive. Besides, you don't owe me anything." She tried to slip it off, but he grasped her hand and held it between his.

"I'm not trying to repay you, Abby. Why would I?" He lifted one eyebrow. "I bought it years ago because I knew you would appreciate it."

And then what—he'd forgotten he had it?

Or he now wanted to be rid of all reminders of the past?

"You can't return a gift, Abby."

"But this—"

"Is yours." He watched her tip her wrist toward the light, as if he understood how little she wanted to give back this bracelet. And he probably did.

Donovan hadn't changed. He was still like a chameleon, spinning dreams and fantasy so well that everyone fell under his spell. But the man himself was impossible to pin down. Only now, seeing him again after so long, did Abby recognize that he'd abandoned the charisma he'd used to skate over life.

"Thank you." Abby undid the clasp and set the bracelet back in its box.

"Abby, about that proposal."

"I'm not going to talk about it, Donovan. It's over. I'm over it. I've moved on. So should you."

"You sound so hard. I don't remember that about you."

She stared straight at him.

"Time and circumstances do that to you, Donovan."

He returned her look without flinching.

"Maybe you should tell me what you think happened that night, Abby," he said, a quiet tension threading his voice. "What did your mother say?"

"What's the point of rehashing that period of our lives? It's over. Now, if you'll excuse me, I need to get back to work." Abby turned her back, pretending to concentrate on her ring.

A few minutes later, she heard the door close.

Her legs weakened and she had to sit down for a minute to regain her equanimity.

So Donovan was back.

"So you avoid him. Keep yourself busy and away from him. He's probably here for only a month or two, anyway. Donovan never sticks to anything anyway." At least not the Donovan she remembered.

For his first week at work, Donovan stuck to his office, familiarizing himself with everything about Weddings by Woodwards. Wednesday night he stayed late, poring over the ad campaigns the company had used in the past.

Puzzled by something he read, Donovan was doing a survey of the sales floor when he saw a light shining in a back room. He checked it out and then wished he'd stayed upstairs.

Abby was hunched over a table, her face determined as she twisted one of the ring's claws tighter.

"It must be tough to find the spare time to do what you love."

"That's life." Abby ignored him.

"Tell me more about this contest." He poked his finger at the fake stone.

"It's for jewelry designers across America who want to reach a broader audience with new designs."

"Meaning the chichi moneyed set?" he pressed on, determined to get rid of the tension between them.

"Meaning people who know jewelry," Abby substituted. "The kind of people I want to know better. In New York."

Donovan detested the snappish self-righteous tone in her voice. He was the good guy here. Five years ago, he'd given her the chance to pursue her dreams.

"You never let anything stand in the way of your goals, do you, Abby?"

"What does that mean?" she demanded, her forehead pleated in a fierce frown. "Do you?"

Donovan sighed. What was he doing—trying to make her admit he'd been right to leave?

"Grandmother says your designs are hot at Woodwards."

"Sales have been going well." She set the ring down before facing him. "Why are you back, Donovan? Are you suddenly interested in the family's wedding planning business?"

Do not take offense, he ordered himself.

"It was time."

"Why now?"

"Grandmother wants a new marketing campaign that will spread the company logo across the country. Something young and hip," he explained. "If the Chicago store goes well, she thinks she might start another on the East Coast, provided I can up our brand recognition to national status. I'm to get to work and earn my keep."

"Oh. No one told me about another store, but then, why would they?"

Donovan winced at the hint that even though Abby had always been like one of the Woodward family when they were dating, there was no reason for them to consider her as part of their inner circle since he'd left. He hadn't considered how that might impact her.

"I heard you were working with one of Winifred's contacts in Paris and enjoying it," she said.

Unasked question: Why leave now?

"I had some changes in my life," he said. "I thought maybe you'd heard."

"Heard what?"

"I brought someone home with me."

"Oh."

"Her name is Ariane."

Something flickered through Abby's expressive eyes, but it was gone so fast he couldn't decipher it.

"She's seven."

"Seven?" Abby blinked.

"I'm her godfather." He saw her disbelief. "Improbable as that may sound, it's the truth."

"I see." Abby kept staring at him.

"She is the daughter of my very best friend. George's death was a shock to all of us." It still hurt to think of that vibrant man silenced in a boating accident. "Ariane's mother died of cancer when she was two. There was no other family. I couldn't leave her a ward of the state. Besides, I'd promised George that I would take care of her."

He paused, collecting his emotions from those horrible weeks.

"I'm very sorry." At least Abby sounded genuine.

"I just wanted you to know. You never seemed like the motherly type, so you probably can't understand my actions, but I knew if I could bring Ariane home, then the family would help her."

"That was very generous of you."

Abby had closed him out. She said the right words, but her heart wasn't in them. She just wasn't interested. Her focus was on her ring.

Like that was unusual. Jewelry had always come first with Abby.

She was packing away her tools.

"Donovan, I've got to go. There are a thousand things on my plate and I'm way past the time I'd allotted for working tonight. Maybe we can talk more another day?"

"Sure." He nodded, watching as she locked her project in a small personal safe near her desk. "Sorry I bothered you."

She didn't say anything and he wondered if she'd even heard. But after a moment she turned, smiling at him.

"Sorry. I had an idea for the contest."

"Totally career focused, as usual." He didn't bother to mask the disparaging tone lacing his words. "It really matters that much to you?"

"Yes, my career matters to me. Just as much as yours does to you," she said, defiant in her own defense. "One way or another, I intend to get my chance in New York."

"I'm sure you will." Irritation chased confusion and a hint of hurt. What had he expected?

"Because you'll be working here, I guess I'll see you around," she said as she flung on her coat. "Will you lock up?"

"I'm leaving now, too. I must get back to Grandmother's. Ariane and I are staying there, for now."

"Oh." Abby trailed behind him to the back door and set the security alarm. But outside, standing on the step, she hesitated.

Donovan didn't know why, so he waited.

"Does it seem weird to be back?" she whispered.

"It seems right," he answered just as quietly. "God used George's death to remind me of how much I need my family and their love and support in my life. Especially now that I'm to care for Ari." He paused to study her. "I hope you can understand that, Abby."

"Understand that family matters? Of course I understand that. Or are you trying to tell me that you're not interested in picking up where we left off five years ago?" Her smile was hard and forced. "Believe me, Donovan, neither am I."

He was making matters worse. Donovan wished he'd never left his office.

"My family is very important to me," he said.

Abby jumped on that.

"So is mine. I might not have the family support that you have, Donovan, but the past five years have taught me one thing." Sparks flew from Abby's hazel eyes.

Donovan opened his mouth, but didn't get a chance to speak.

"If I'm going to get to New York, I'm going to have to do it on my own. Alone."

With that she walked away into the night.

Chapter Two

Abby's words helped Donovan decide his course of action.

He would avoid her as much as possible while he figured out how to do his job and be a father to Ariane. Maybe later, somewhere along the way, he'd figure out a way to breach the chasm between them without getting caught up in the past.

It was a fine decision.

Unfortunately, his grandmother blew it out of the water on Thursday evening when she called him into the living room after he'd tucked in Ariane.

"Sit down, dear. I made some coffee."

"You're not supposed to be drinking coffee." He shook his head at her. "And don't say it's for me. I don't drink coffee this late at night."

"I'm allowed this much." Winifred liberally laced her half cup with cream. "Have you settled in? Ariane's all right?"

"We're fine, Grandmother. Thank you for hosting us." She had something on her mind. He could see it in the sparks lighting her eyes. "I hope we're not putting you out too much."

"I'll let you know when you do." She tapped the spoon on her saucer twice before she set it down and leaned forward.

"You and Abby talked? There aren't going to be any problems between you?"

Not if he stayed away from her.

"Well, after five years, it was a little difficult to squeeze everything into a couple of fifteen-minute discussions," he temporized. "But I've apologized and Abby said she didn't want to hark back to the past. We're both professionals. I think we can do our jobs at Weddings by Woodwards without conflict."

"I see." Winifred leaned back and sipped her coffee, her eagle eyes trained on him. "You never did clarify why you left town so quickly after proposing to the girl."

And he wasn't going to explain now.

"First you announced your engagement and then, bang, you were on the next flight to Europe, a job for which you had already turned me down." Clearly Winifred wanted an explanation.

"I—uh, realized I'd made a mistake. So I corrected it."

"The way you did it seemed kind of hard on Abby."

"What did she say?" Donovan asked curiously.

"Abby?" Winifred shook her head. "Nothing to me. I overheard an argument between her and her mother that grad night. The next day, I learned she'd left for a short holiday. When she came back, she moved into her own place, put a smile on her lips and focused on whatever work I assigned her."

"For the summer, you mean." Just as he'd done, Donovan thought.

"From then until now. Abby's never left Woodwards."

Donovan sat up, confused.

"But what about when she went to college?"

"Abby didn't go to college." Winifred frowned. "She's taken a number of courses over the past few years, of course. She's fully qualified as a jewelry designer. But she never formally attended college. She's always focused on her work."

"Because her career is so important to her." For five years

Donovan had prayed hard for the bitterness to leave. Guess that needed more work.

"I'm not sure that was true back then. She seemed to need the work to give herself focus five years ago." Winifred smiled. "But she's certainly career-oriented now. Not that I'm complaining. Abby is the best thing to happen to our jewelry department."

Something didn't make sense. Abby had won a full college scholarship. Why hadn't she gone?

Winifred set down her cup.

"Actually, Abby is why I wanted to speak to you, Donovan."

"Oh?" Trepidation climbed up his neck.

"I know that girl is going places. She has the drive and she has the capability. Before she does, I want to use her skills, and yours, to make some changes in our jewelry department. I want the two of you to come up with some kind of campaign or re-vamping of ideas—something that will give Woodwards Jewelry a whole new look. In short, I want you two to work together."

Donovan went cold.

"Grandmother, you've already asked me to put together a national campaign. I'm not sure I can manage that and—"

"Aren't you the marketing guru who said he had a thousand ideas?" Winifred's perceptive gaze narrowed. "I want the jewelry department modernized, Donovan. If two projects are too much for you, we'll put the national one on hold."

She was shrewd. Donovan knew there was no way to avoid this assignment without admitting to his grandmother that he'd never resolved exactly how he felt toward Abby.

"Unless there's some reason why you can't work with her." Those all-seeing eyes dared him to argue.

"If that's what you want, Grandmother, then that is what I'll work toward. I can't help thinking though, that Abby is already swamped. And now she's entered this contest." He told her what little he knew about it. "With her parents' situation, I know she's struggling to fit in enough time to work on her first entry."

Donovan slouched into his chair and fiddled with his shoelace, pretending nonchalance.

"I'm glad she's entered it," Winifred said with satisfaction. "She has talent. Loads of it."

"Of course preparing for the New York contest will be on her own time, but still, it's a lot to ask of her to help revamp her department right now, isn't it?" Donovan said.

Winifred was not put off.

"You and Abby are both idea people. I'm sure that with your creative gifts combined you'll come up with something fantastic." Winifred sipped her coffee, closing her eyes to savor the last drop. Then she reluctantly set cup and saucer back on the tray. "One of the things I most regret about this old heart wearing out is cutting down on my coffee."

Because he could see weariness creeping over her smooth porcelain face, Donovan stifled the other arguments he'd lined up.

"When would you like us to start?" he asked quietly.

"The sooner the better. Perhaps you can talk to Abby about it tomorrow, do some preliminary work. She's been in charge of the department long enough, I'm certain she has ideas of her own. It shouldn't take more than a couple of weeks to put together some kind of generalized plan, should it?"

Two weeks? That left him no opportunity to avoid Abby. Donovan searched for some excuse to explain the intricacies of his work to Winifred and realized there wasn't any point. Only someone who had spent days, weeks and months knitting ideas together into one solid focus would understand that overnight successes of the marketing variety seldom happened.

"I think it's better if you don't put a time frame on it, Grand-mother. I don't know what ideas Abby might have, but I will need time to take a look at the department. I always like to allow things to percolate inside my head before I start planning a campaign." Donovan watched her eyes narrow and knew what she was thinking. "I'm not trying to weasel out of this or to put you off. But I hadn't really considered any kind of marketing plan for the jewelry department. I've been focusing more on the company in general."

"And you need time to switch gears," she murmured.

"Yes."

Her stare was intense.

"You're sure it's not working with Abby that has you bothered?"

"Why should it be? I hope we can be friends again, but there's nothing between us. We each have our own lives now and my focus is on Ariane." Donovan forced out the image of Abby storming away from him.

Avoiding her shouldn't be that difficult.

"However, I do think it would be better if you explained this idea to her, rather than me," Donovan suggested. "After all, I'm the new guy and you're the boss returning to work after a long hiatus. You should be pointing out the new direction for the company."

Winifred said nothing as she studied him. But Donovan could almost hear her clicking over details in her mind.

"Fine. I'll talk to her. I just hope your past isn't going to cause problems."

"You don't have to worry, Grandmother."

But as he sat in his room later, Donovan's confidence slipped. Although he preferred to pretend the past was dead, it was obvious he and Abby both had issues that needed resolving.

Abby might prefer to pretend their breakup was his fault, but he knew differently and he didn't understand why she tried to lay it all on him. A hard core of resentment balled a little tighter inside Donovan's heart.

But bitterness did no one any good. George's death had been God's wake-up call, a challenge to stop wasting his life as a good-times guy, skating over the surface, reveling in the good times and avoiding the bad.

Donovan was determined not to ignore that call anymore. He picked up his Bible and read a few verses, hoping to ease the knot of anger at Abby's pretense that he'd run out on her with no reason. But the words blurred together and he knew there was only one Person who could truly help.

"Father, you know how hard it was for me to come back. You also know how much I need help with Ariane. Please help me to look forward to the future you promised, and let go of the past and anger at Abby. Amen."

As prayers went, it wasn't fancy, but Donovan was learning that God preferred honesty over pretense.

He wished Abby felt the same.

"Abby, I can't thank you enough for helping me decorate for Grandmother's party."

"My pleasure." Abby attached the last swag to the corner of the dais and ignored a little voice inside her head that said she should be working on her contest entry. "How does that look?"

"Perfect!" Sara, Donovan's youngest sister, stood back and admired their handiwork in the ballroom at Weddings by Woodwards. "Once Dad brings in his flowers and everyone's here, the place will come alive. Don't you think?"

"Absolutely." Abby felt dumpy and dowdy, doubly so against Sara's blond glistening beauty.

"Donovan took us all by surprise, coming home the way he did." Sara grinned. "He's always been so adamant about staying in Europe. But I'm glad he's back. And I'm thrilled Grandmother's well enough to return, too. My big sister is getting too intense," she whispered as Katie pushed through the doors.

"I heard that, brat." Katie made a face at Sara, then turned to her. "Abby, how is your mother?"

"She'll be sore for a while. The osteoporosis has really left her bones weak which is why her vertebrae crushed so easily when she fell down the steps." Which only added to the list of things on Abby's already overly full plate. "Thanks for under-standing about yesterday, Katie. I just couldn't get in."

"Of course not. Family comes first." Katie scanned the room. "Wow! You two have done a wonderful job for our double celebration tonight. We'll be a big group. I've given the kitchen staff the evening off so they can join us."

"So who's feeding us?" Sara demanded.

"Caterers. They should be here soon."

"That's my cue to get going." Abby headed for the door.

"Going? But you'll be here for the party, won't you?" Sara's big eyes probed.

"Won't you, Abby?" Katie asked.

"Sure. I just have a few things on my desk to tidy up." And then she'd quietly slip away.

"You're always working overtime. Katie won't care if you take the last hour to go home and change. Will you, Katie?"

"Of course not. You must be here, Abby. You're part of Woodwards. Excuse me. I'm to check on a certain string quartet Grandmother loves." Katie hurried away.

"Thank goodness she's gone. My feet are killing me."

"I wonder why?" Abby chuckled, glancing at the very high heels Sara wore. "You borrowed Katie's shoes again?"

"My sister has such lovely shoes and they make me look elegant, which is not an easy feat, trust me. But they're sheer torture. I can't imagine how she wears them all day." She kicked off the offending articles with great relief. "That's better."

"Sara, if you don't like the way the shoes feel, why do you wear them?" Abby had always found Donovan's youngest sister confusing.

"Because I want to look beautiful for my husband." Sara's flushed cheeks and eyes glittering with unshed tears gave her away. "Although if I trip and fall flat on my face, I guess I won't be so elegant. And he'll be furious."

"Furious? That doesn't sound right. Cade loves you." A twig of envy sprouted inside Abby's heart. "Very much. I can't believe he'd be angry with you."

"He does love me and I know it." Sara sniffed inelegantly. "But in a little while I'll be so huge I won't be able to see my toenails, let alone fit into shoes like these. Just for now I want to be the most beautiful woman he's ever seen."

"You're expecting," Abby guessed. "Oh, my."

"You can say that again. I'm over the moon, but sick as a dog every morning. Not very romantic, you'll agree?" Sara tried to smile, but frustration took precedence. "I feel horrible most of the time and I grouch at Cade about everything. Today I wanted to look extra pretty, but now my feet hurt so much I can hardly walk."

She burst into tears.

As Abby patted her shoulder, she marveled at this beautiful Woodward daughter's uncertainty. She had everything and yet she was still upset. Abby had to help.

"Come on, let's go see what's in the shoe department." When Sara tried to slide her feet into the heels, Abby snatched them up. "Give me those," she scolded.

When they arrived at the shoe department, Abby took the sales assistant aside and explained the situation.

"I know the exact thing. Keep her sitting there. I'll be back in a couple of minutes."

Sara lay sprawled in her chair, eyes closed, obviously resting. Abby examined her own reflection in the mirror opposite and wished she hadn't. She was dusty, part of her hem was loose and the shirt that had been pristine this morning looked tired.

Not exactly party material.

She caught sight of a rich red dress in the next department and longed to try it on. Just looking at it made her feel lighter, prettier, younger.

"How about these?" The shoe salesman held a pair of wedge-heeled shoes that, while flattering the ankle, didn't have the wobbling height of Sara's borrowed stilettos.

"Perfect," Abby whispered. "Now how do we get her to wear them?"

"I can hear you talking about me, you know." Sara tried on the shoes and asked to have them put on her account. "What are you staring at?"

Abby turned away, but she was too late.

"That dress is perfect for you, Abby. You haven't got time to go home and change now anyway because of me." Sara frowned. "Unless—do you have to do something for your parents about dinner?"

"No. It's all taken care of." Her parents thought she was working. And she'd intended to be. But she hadn't known about the welcome-back party when she'd said that. She gave the dress another wistful glance.

Wouldn't it be wonderful to wear a dress like that? But buying the dress would take a bite out of the savings she needed for gems for her project.

"I can't afford it," she said to quell Sara's urging.

"Yes, you can. It's on the forty percent–off rack. Come on, Abby. Tonight's a celebration."

Once she had tried the dress on, Abby knew she couldn't give it up.

Sara agreed.

"It's perfect."

"I think so, too." Abby giggled. "Stop pushing. I'll take it already."

"Good. You deserve to do something nice for yourself once in a while." Sara's phone pealed. "Hi, honey," she said into it, her face a wreath of smiles. "I'm helping Abby pick out a dress. Yes, I'd love to go for a drive. Why don't we take the twins? It would give Olivia a breather. In fact, tell her to trade places with me. Abby might try and put this dress back and she shouldn't. Olivia will persuade her."

Sara's obvious joy in talking to her husband carved a little jealous hole in Abby's heart. How wonderful to feel so loved, so precious to someone else without feeling you had to earn it. Sara wore the same glow that Abby saw in Reese Woodward's eyes whenever he looked at Olivia, his new wife. Abby could only imagine what it was like to have someone with whom to share her life, to feel his support when you stretched to reach your goals.

Sara shut off her phone.

"I'm going for a ride with Cade and the twins," she said, her voice breathless, as if she couldn't wait.

"Congratulations again. You haven't told anyone about the baby yet?"

"No, and we'd really appreciate it if you'd keep our secret for a little while longer, Abby. We're going to tell the family tonight."

"They'll be ecstatic." Amid the family's excitement over this momentous event, no one would even notice what she wore, Abby was sure. But she refused to give up the dress. There was something about wearing it that made her feel as if she could fit in anywhere, as if she didn't have to try so hard to prove herself.

A minute later, Olivia arrived, breathless and laughing as she hugged Sara first, then Abby.

"That is the most fantastic dress, Abby," she enthused. "You're a knockout."

"Thanks. With this new project I'm working on, I might even get to wear it a second time."

"What project?"

"I'll show you, if you want."

"Olivia! You're supposed to take her mind off work," Sara scolded. "I have to go." She touched her lips to each of their cheeks, then hurried away in her new shoes, glowing like a bride.

"She looks so happy." Jealousy tugged at Abby.

"She is. God did a wonderful thing when he put Sara and Cade together." Olivia followed Abby to her office. "What are these?" she asked, looking at a tray on a cart.

"Beads. I sometimes fool around with them when I'm trying to come up with a design." Abby pushed the cart against the wall, out of the way, before she showed Olivia her ideas for the contest.

Olivia oohed and ahhed over Abby's preliminary sketches. "Very ambitious. I know you'll win."

"Thank you."

"It's a lovely design for a ring. Is it for someone special?"

"Yes. A consignment that I want to use as my project centerpiece."

"How do you come up with ideas like this?"

Abby had just begun to explain when she realized Olivia's attention had drifted to something behind her.

"Hello." Olivia's voice softened. "I'm Olivia. This is Abby. You must be Ariane."

A young girl stood in the doorway, dark head nodding. Abby caught a flash of interest in the wide brown eyes when they rested on the little cart full of beads. One slender hand reached out to touch the yellow ones.

"Would you like to make something?" Abby offered. She drew a roll of wire from the drawer and cut off a six-inch length.

Ariane frowned at her and backed away as if afraid.

"I'd like to make something," Olivia murmured. She drew two chairs forward, one obviously for Ariane. She sat down, then picked up the wire. "What do you do now, Abby?"

"It's very simple. Choose the beads you like and thread them onto the wire. Like this." Abby demonstrated, peeking to see if Ariane was watching. She was.

"I can do that." Olivia slipped two on the wire, but then hesitated. "I don't know what to do next," she said with a wink at Abby. "Should I choose red or blue?"

Abby remained silent, pretending to be perplexed. After a moment, Ariane stepped forward, picked up one red and one blue bead and slid them on, placing a white one between.

"You're absolutely right. That's perfect. Thank you, Ariane."

Ariane nodded. She smiled at Abby, then turned and left.

"Well, that was interesting." Abby put back the beading tray. "I guess she's here waiting for Donovan."

"She looked lonely. I'm going to see if she's all right." Olivia hurried away.

Abby stared at the little bracelet Ariane had begun. She added a few twists, some bigger beads and little closures on the end. She laid the finished product on the cart. It was too girly for Olivia's twin boys. Maybe she'd give it to Ariane if she came back.

"Donovan has her. She's a sweet child." Olivia picked up the bracelet, shook her head. "I had no idea you could create something like this out of beads. It's lovely."

"I only embellished on the red, white and blue theme she started," Abby demurred, an idea flickering through her mind for her own collection.

"Ariane looked so defenseless that I wanted to hug her and reassure her that she's not alone. She has a great big new family now. Of course, that would overwhelm her and I don't want to do that, but as soon as I can, I'm going to have a chat with Ariane. Maybe I can slip in a few words about God."

"God?" Abby's confusion must have shown.

"You know, how God is always on our side. That we can always count on him. That we're never alone," Olivia prodded.

"Oh. Yes. That might reassure her."

"You're not really with me, are you, Abby? I can see you're itching to get your fingers working." Olivia grinned. "Go ahead. I need to talk to Reese, anyway. See you later?"

"Sure." But Abby didn't hear her leave. Her brain was too busy rehashing Olivia's words.

God is always on our side. We can always count on him.
Was Olivia right?

Abby decided to take another look through the Bible that Donovan's mother had given her last Christmas.

It would be nice to have somebody on her side.

Chapter Three

"Waiting for someone special, brother dear?"

Donovan studied his baby sister. Sara sparkled with happiness as she flitted around him like a pesky mosquito.

"Like maybe—Abby?"

Sara's husband, Cade Porter, lounged a few feet away, ostensibly listening to Donovan's mother chatter about something at work. But the man's protective stance told Donovan that the tall, lean cowboy would know exactly where his wife was at any given moment this evening. Cade and Sara had been flashing secret messages back and forth with their eyes ever since they'd arrived.

"Let it go, pest." He'd never get a better time to apologize. "I'm really sorry I missed your wedding, Sara. I should have been here and I wasn't. I let you down because I let business overwhelm me. That was a stupid thing to do and I wish I hadn't."

"I was very mad at you for a while, Donovan." Sara pouted for a minute, then smiled. "Very mad."

"I deserve it."

"But Cade pointed out that you'd be coming home someday and then I could get payback at my leisure. Which I will," she promised. "Cade is a smart man."

"Yeah, he seems okay. A little too ready to pounce maybe, but nice."

"He's wonderful. I love him and we're very happy."

"I can tell. You deserve happiness, Sara, and I hope you and Cade get it in spades." Donovan hugged her close, wishing he hadn't missed everything. Which was odd for him. Regrets were not a usual part of his life.

"I like Ariane," Sara said as she drew away. "She's a sweetheart, but I wish she'd loosen up. She looks so scared."

"If you had this family thrown at you all at once, you'd be a little scared, too. Give her time and she'll be fine." I hope. "In the meantime, I think I'd better rescue her from Brett and Brady. They make me afraid and I'm not a little girl."

"No, when it comes to women, you're a big chicken, brother dear."

Sara's laughter followed him across the room. Donovan gave his father the high sign and soon Brett and Brady, Reese's rambunctious twins, had left Ariane to regale their grandfather with tales of their afternoon at Cade and Sara's ranch.

"Everything okay, Ari?" he whispered.

She said nothing, simply nodded. He might have been a complete stranger for all the attention she paid him.

"Hey, everyone." Fiona's voice cut through the hum of noise like a paper shredder. His mother had never required amplification. "Abby's here."

It had been easy to avoid Abby on Thursday because she was away. Donovan had stayed away all day Friday out of sheer busyness. But he wouldn't be able to keep it up forever. They would have to work together sooner or later.

But that wasn't why he sought her out now. Tonight he was going to introduce her to Ariane because he wanted the little girl to meet all of the people who worked at Woodwards.

"There's someone I want to introduce you to," Donovan whispered.

Ariane grabbed his hand and held on, fear filling her expressive eyes.

"Don't worry. You'll like her." He straightened, glanced toward the door and gulped as if he'd been swamped by one of the waves off Big Sur.

Abby had always been pretty, but tonight she was stunning. Her streaked hair usually fell to her shoulders, thick and straight. Tonight it was drawn up on her head, adding to her height. Slim and graceful in a red dress that hinted at her femininity and offered a glimpse of elegant legs, she looked like a fashion model. Sparkling stones nestled into her earlobes as if they'd grown there. On one wrist she wore the bracelet he'd given her on Thursday.

This was not his old school pal.

"I'm so glad you're back," Abby said to Winifred, right before she hugged her.

"Thank you, dear." Winifred touched her chin. "You look lovely."

"It's one of your creations. How could I not?"

"I want to know about this New York project you're working on."

"Of course. Any time." Abby turned, saw him. "Hello, Donovan," she said, her voice as cool as an Arctic breeze.

"Hi, Abby." His throat felt swollen, like a school boy's. He drew Ariane forward to hide his sudden attack of nerves. "I want you to meet someone. Ariane, this is Abby."

He'd been going to say, "my friend," but dropped it at the last second.

"We've already met. Ariane stopped by a little earlier to check out my beads. Hello." Abby stretched out her hand and gently shook Ariane's. "Next time when you come we'll make something really pretty. Okay?"

The little girl regarded Abby solemnly for several moments before nodding.

"You're always welcome," Abby told her with a smile, though it was clear she wondered why Ariane didn't speak.

Brady and Brett came rushing up to invite Ariane to taste the punch. After a quick silent check with Donovan, Ariane followed, at a much slower pace.

"I hope she didn't get in your way, Abby."

"Of course not. She was just curious."

"I should have told you this before but—" There was no easy way to say it. "Ariane doesn't speak. She hasn't since she witnessed her father's accident. He was water skiing and another boat hit him. The doctors say it will take time before she feels able to talk again."

"Oh, the poor thing." Compassion glittered in Abby's pretty eyes. "I wish there was something I could do to help her."

Donovan frowned. A five-year-old conversation returned.

Abby detests kids. She puts on a good front, but she's not interested in the things other girls are, like family. She's totally focused on her future.

Could she have changed that much?

"We checked out her school this afternoon. She's to start Monday morning."

"I'm sure she'll fit in beautifully." Abby's cool look was back. "You'll do fine, Donovan. Excuse me. I want to speak to Sara."

"Sure."

Abby hurried toward his sister. The two shared a laugh before Cade offered them each a glass of the cranberry punch Winifred adored. Donovan felt as if Abby deliberately avoided looking at him when she turned to speak to Olivia.

"You're frowning, Donovan. Is something wrong?" Winifred studied him with the same eagle eye she used to employ when he was a toddler in her Sunday school class. Her glance tracked to Abby.

"Nothing's wrong." One look told him she wasn't satisfied with that response. "It's just a bit awkward with Abby."

"Bound to be, I imagine. You asked the girl to marry you, after all." Winifred gave him a dark look. "Then you welshed on the deal. Still, you're both adults now, pursuing your own careers. I'm sure you can get past it. Can't you?"

The real question was, would he let the past influence the future?

"She seems so different."

"Five years changes everyone. Including you. Now come over here. I want you to meet someone." Her voice softened. "This is Art Woodward. He's your grandfather's stepbrother."

"I didn't know he had one. Nice to meet you, Art." Donovan shook the older man's hand and noticed how quickly the man's other palm encircled Winifred's waist.

"Neither did we know until recently. But we're so glad Art's here. He owns part of the local television station. He's just come back from buying another in Tucson," Winifred said.

"Well, that may come in handy for my publicity campaign," Donovan teased. But his brain filed the look on his grandmother's face, the way Art smiled at her, the sense of togetherness the two projected.

"Let me know what you need, Donovan, and I'll aim to provide it," Art told him. "But not tonight. This is a party and I want the first dance with this beautiful lady."

Art and Winifred walked to the dance floor and slid into each other's arms as if they'd been a couple for years. As they glided around the room, Donovan couldn't help but admit they looked good together.

"What do you think of him?" Reese asked quietly.

"I don't know what to think. Is he always that…friendly with Grandmother?"

"Pretty much. They've seen a lot of each other ever since he arrived and more so since she had her operation. She seems to adore him."

"Who'd have thought?" Donovan looked for and found Ariane. She stood in a corner, sipping punch, her attention on Abby who was smiling and gesturing as she talked.

"Made your amends there yet?" Reese asked.

"I apologized. Abby said it didn't matter, that she'd moved on."

"You believe it?"

"I don't know what to think. She's changed a lot. More focused. Harder." Donovan shrugged. "Not that it matters. I don't have time for anything but my work here and Ariane."

"Are you trying to convince me or yourself?" Reese held up a hand. "I don't need an answer. But if you want to talk, I'm available. It's good to have you back, little brother."

"Thanks, Reese. I hope I can share some of the burden for this place."

"Just don't make the same mistake I did in thinking work is the panacea for pain." Reese clapped a hand on his shoulder. "Take it from me, it isn't. Think I'll go dance with my wife."

"You do that. Olivia's a beautiful woman. You're a lucky man."

Reese shook his head.

"Not lucky," he said firmly. "Blessed."

Donovan watched him nudge Olivia, then murmur something in her ear. She smiled and inclined her head toward the twins who were staring at the welcome-back cake that sat on a stand at the front of the room. Reese looked as if he'd go and get them, but Olivia shook her head and lifted her hand to his shoulder. They stepped onto the floor with the comfort of two people who understood each other.

Winifred, with Art in tow, touched Donovan's shoulder, drawing his attention to his parents. He watched his laughing mother tease his grimacing father, who was not following her lead on the dance floor.

"Everyone seems to have a partner but you," Winifred murmured. "Why don't you ask Abby to dance?"

"She doesn't dance," he said, and then wondered if that was

still true. So many things he'd thought he knew for certain had changed. Abby dancing was probably the least of them.

"Even if that's so, it would still be nice to ask her."

"It would be a little awkward, don't you think, Grandmother? Dating isn't in my future and I'm pretty sure Abby's focused on her contest."

"You don't have to date her," Winifred sniffed. "But it might be nice if you two could get rid of the barriers."

"We've done that already." Because he was watching Winifred so closely, Donovan saw the slight rose flush that colored her delicately powdered cheeks. "Don't matchmake, Grandmother. Whatever was between Abby and me in high school died five years ago."

"I wouldn't dream of matchmaking," Winifred sniffed. "I know you're trying to be responsible. I know you're working hard to be a good father to Ariane and I applaud you. But being a father can't and shouldn't become your whole life. Reese can tell you about that." Winifred asked Art for some punch, then threaded her arm through Donovan's and drew him toward a table where he helped her sit.

"Are you all right?" he asked, worried by her pale color.

"I'm fine. Listen to me. Abby's become as precious to me as if she was my own granddaughter. I want her to achieve all of her dreams. I believe she has the capacity to reach great heights."

"So do I," he agreed.

"I don't want her to feel awkward about working here just because you're back, Donovan."

"I don't think Abby's that easily upset," he murmured, watching as she danced with the twins, laughing at their antics. So she did dance.

Abby detests kids. It hadn't rung true then and it didn't now. Her eyes sparkled with fun, her smile spread across her face.

"Abby hides her feelings. She's had to. Talk to God, Donovan. Find out how he wants you to respond to Abby."

Having said her piece, Winifred signaled Katie who asked everyone to have a seat. Donovan beckoned Ariane to sit beside him as the others all found places. Art sat next to Winifred.

When the room was silent again, Katie took the microphone.

"Welcome to our welcome-back party," she said, grinning. "It is our greatest pleasure to have Grandmother with us tonight and my special pleasure to tell you that come Monday morning, she expects to be seated behind her desk, making sure we're all hard at work."

The room erupted in cheering. Katie waited until there was relative silence.

"Dad?"

Thomas Woodward rose, lifted his glass.

"I'd like to propose a toast to my mother. May she be behind that desk for years to come. Welcome back, Winifred."

"To Winifred."

Donovan tinkled his glass against Ariane's and waited for her to taste the apple cider. She wrinkled her nose after a sip, but gamely gave it another try. Katie turned to him.

"My brother Donovan has at long last returned from Europe to head up our own in-house marketing department. We're glad he's back and thrilled he brought his goddaughter Ariane with him. Welcome home, Donovan and Ariane."

Slightly embarrassed, Donovan rose, bowed and promised he'd do his best for Weddings by Woodwards while Ariane stared at everyone with her huge dark eyes. Finally, Fiona rose to say a blessing over the food. When Donovan looked up, Abby had slipped into the seat across from them.

"There wasn't anywhere else," she apologized in a whisper.

"No problem."

"I saw Winifred talking to you earlier. Is she all right?"

"She's fine." He waited until their salads had been served. "Ariane's been admiring you."

"Oh." Abby blinked, then glanced at his goddaughter. "Why?"

"I think it's your earrings. She loves all that sparkles. Your design?"

Abby nodded.

"They're lovely."

"Thanks." She averted her eyes and concentrated on eating.

"Abby makes lots of jewelry, Ari. She's a quite-famous jewelry designer."

"Not yet, but soon, hopefully." Abby smiled at Ariane who seemed intrigued by the bracelet Donovan had given Abby. "Do you like jewelry, Ariane?"

The little girl nodded eagerly and after signaling that she needed a pen from Donovan, she drew an altered picture of the bracelet she'd helped Olivia form.

"Ah, I see you've had a change of idea. That's what we designers do." Abby smiled at her. "The bracelet's in my office, waiting for you."

Ariane seemed happy to hear that and settled down to dinner, like everyone else. Donovan couldn't reconcile the easy camaraderie she and Abby shared, with what he'd been told. As the meal drew to a finish, his suspicions about that conversation multiplied, but Donovan stuffed them away and focused on enjoying the evening.

Reese took his turn as MC. Sara sang a song about homecomings and Cade announced their pregnancy. Once congratulations had died down, Katie had her parents act out a charade about the Chicago store.

Donovan took it all in like a bystander and realized that his sisters, his brother, Grandmother, his parents were all genuinely enjoying life, friends and family. Only he felt as if he had to work to smile. Even though Ariane was beside him and Abby across from him, even though the room was full of his family, he suddenly felt lonely. In that moment, he realized something else.

Abby wasn't the only one with a pressing goal.

He wanted to be an integral part of his family's lives now. He wanted to be the one they turned to when they needed to talk things over, the one they called on when they needed a shoulder to lean on. He wanted to be the son they counted on.

The prospect both terrified and tantalized Donovan. He'd never been good with long-term anything, especially commitment, although he'd wanted to try with Abby. A few hours talking to God might help him figure out how to become more than the carefree role he'd always defined for himself.

Maybe then Abby wouldn't look at him with that funny little smile that clearly said she felt sorry for him for having missed so much.

Chapter Four

Monday mornings were always hectic.

Today leaned more toward crazy.

Anticipating the furor, Abby had arrived early. She filed her approved sketch for a newly commissioned diamond engagement ring, made changes another customer had requested on an anniversary ring and released the delicate tiara she'd created for a local fashion show.

Then she allowed herself a coffee break and a few moments to study the ring she wanted to send in for her contest entry. It was almost ready. A tweak or two and—

A child's wail erupted from the front of the store. Assuming it was Brett or Brady, both of whom knew exactly how to create disaster at Weddings by Woodwards, Abby hurried toward the sound. She found Donovan kneeling in front of Ariane, his face taut with worry.

"It's okay, Ari. Just tell me what's wrong? Are you sick?"

One negative head jerk.

"Is it your clothes? But this is the school's uniform."

Ariane wailed a little more. Only it wasn't really a wail. More like a soft, mewling cry.

"Honey, if you'll just tell me what's wrong, I'll fix it. Do your shoes hurt?" Another shake of that dark glossy head left Donovan looking completely mystified and adorably uncertain.

Although she longed to ignore them both, Abby had to help.

"Hello, Ariane. Donovan. Can I help?"

"I don't think so, thanks, Abby. Something's wrong, but—" He stopped as Ariane walked over and threaded her hand into Abby's. "Oh."

"I have some drawing crayons in my office," Abby mused. "Why don't you come and draw me a picture while we figure out what's got you so upset?"

Ariane nodded and after a reproachful look at Donovan, walked beside Abby to her office. Seated in a chair, she waited until Abby handed her crayons and some paper. Then her eyes moved to Abby's ring for the contest. She poked at it curiously, picked it up and slid it on her finger.

Donovan stepped forward as if to stop her, but Abby rested a hand on his arm.

"Wait," she murmured.

Ariane studied the ring for several moments. Then she put it back and began drawing a representation of it but with added swirls that resembled a flower circling the stone. It took Abby several moments to recognize a gardenia—Winifred's favorite flower. Did the girl know Art had commissioned the ring for Winifred?

Ariane held up the paper for her to see.

"It's lovely. May I use it in my design?"

Ariane nodded.

"Good. Now, tell me what's wrong." Judging by Ariane's frown, this was touchy territory. Abby got the ball rolling. "Today's your first day of school, isn't it?"

The little girl nodded while big tears dripped down her cheeks.

"But that's not a sad time. School is fun. You'll see." Abby hunched down beside her. "There are lots of books. Do you know how to read?"

Ariane nodded, sniffed.

"She loves stories," Donovan added.

"And there's playtime. And craft time. You'll be good at that." She touched the girl's cheek, dabbed at her tears. "You'll learn lots and lots of new fun things. I did."

Ariane grabbed another paper. *Did you wear a uniform?* she printed in a childish scrawl.

"Yes. So did Donovan."

Ariane tilted her head to see if it was true.

"Abby's was always clean. Mine got a little dingy." His funny face made Ariane giggle.

"I suspect you'll be very popular at school, Ariane. Just like Donovan was."

"Abby always got the best marks. She beat me in spelling. But I beat her in baseball." Donovan winked at Ariane who glanced from him to Abby, her confusion evident.

"We got to be friends. When you go to school, you'll find a friend, too. Wouldn't that be fun?"

Ariane's bottom lip thrust out. Abby glanced at Donovan. But he was clearly confused by the girl's distress and couldn't help. Abby tried again.

"Wouldn't you like to go just to see who's there?" She crossed her fingers.

Ariane shook her head.

"But how can you know what might happen if you never try something?" Abby wasn't sure how to approach this. Being an only child didn't offer a lot of knowledge about kids.

"Keep going," Donovan urged.

Abby shot him a glare. As if she didn't have enough to do. But suddenly she had an idea.

"Do you like ice cream, Ariane?"

Ariane nodded eagerly.

"You had to eat an ice-cream cone first to know you liked it, right? It's the same with school," Abby said.

Ariane's glowering glare said she wasn't buying Abby's train of thought.

Abby looked to Donovan for help. Worry colored his eyes and spread fine lines over his forehead. He would be no help.

"What flavors of ice cream do you like?"

Ariane drew a cone with ice cream with brown dots.

"Chocolate chip?" Abby grinned when the child nodded. "What other kinds?"

Ariane frowned, poked at the cone she'd drawn.

"Yeah, I know. But there are lots more ice-cream flavors than that. I often try a new one, just in case I might find something better than butter pecan. It's my favorite." Abby picked up a crayon and drew a cone with a pink top. "Strawberry. Peach. Fudge, they're all pretty good, but butter pecan is the best. Do you like these flavors?"

Ariane pointed to the fudge and the strawberry.

"You don't like peach?"

Ariane's shrug said she'd never tried it.

"I like peach. And pistachio. That's my favorite." Donovan was getting into the game. "Do you like pistachio, Ari?"

She frowned, thought about it then half shook her head no.

"How do you know?" Abby asked. "Did you try some?"

The little girl crossed her arms across her thin chest, leaned back and glared at them both. She wasn't going to be easily persuaded. Abby didn't want to alienate her, but she had to emphasize what she might miss, so she pressed on.

"I know two boys, your cousins, who love bubblegum ice cream. Lots of kids do. You probably would, too," Abby mused, "if you tried some. Just as you'd like school, if you tried it."

The dark head gave a very emphatic negative shake.

"Really? You're sure about that?"

Ariane wasn't backing down.

"You're positive? You won't change your mind and love it later?"

Ariane's head moved from side to side as her jaw tightened. "I don't think that's true. I think you're afraid."

Donovan caught his breath and shifted, but Abby stepped sideways so Ariane couldn't see him. She kept speaking.

"I think you're terrified, Ariane. And I don't like that. You know why?" She waited a moment. "Because being afraid isn't a good enough reason to miss out on stuff. So here's what I'm going to do. I'm going to dare you to go to your first day of school. I'm going to double dare you to go and meet the other kids and the teachers and go to all the classes. What do you think of that?"

It was a gamble that the child would understand the concept of a dare, but it paid off. Clearly Ariane got it. She glared at Abby, but her face showed she was listening. Abby crouched down in front of her and took one hand, folding it into her own.

"I can't imagine someone who comes to Denver all the way from Paris can possibly be afraid of school. You have schools in Paris, don't you?"

Ariane nodded.

"And I bet some kids wear uniforms to them, too, don't they?"

Another nod.

"In fact, you're pretty experienced and school isn't such a big deal for you at all." Abby let the words drop away in the room's silence watching as Ariane's shoulders lifted in growing confidence.

Her big brown eyes studied Abby for several moments more. Finally, Ariane pulled her hand from Abby's, walked over to Donovan and put her tiny hand in his.

"So you're taking my dare?" Abby kept her face impassive as Ariane nodded. "Okay. So if you're wrong and you do like school, I win a huge ice cream cone. Butter pecan. And you have to buy it, right?"

Ariane glanced at Donovan and rolled her eyes as if to say "Adults are so lame."

"Yep, that's the deal." Donovan winked at Ariane.

"And if I'm wrong and Ariane doesn't like the school, I'll have to buy her a different flavored ice-cream cone for the next four Saturdays. Agreed?"

Donovan nodded, but Ariane's confidence was clearly wobbling.

Abby faked a frown.

"You know, just to make sure you two don't try and pull one over on me and pretend you win, I think I better go along and see for myself. Buying so many ice creams could be costly and I don't want to work any more overtime."

"Abby, that isn't necess—"

Ariane grabbed her backpack. The thunderclouds dissipated from her face.

"I don't believe this." Donovan shook his head. "Now you're ready to go?"

She nodded, grinned.

"Never turn down a dare, huh?"

She scribbled *I like choc'lat ice cream.*

"Tell me something I don't know." He sighed, shook his head. "If you're sure you can spare the time, Abby, let's go. School starts soon."

No backing out now. Abby grabbed her purse and followed them after locking her office door. On the ride to the school, she told silly jokes she'd overheard Brett and Brady regale their sister Emily with. That seemed to help Ariane forget the miles for a time.

She glowered when they pulled into the parking lot, but with one little hand firmly embedded in Donovan's and one in Abby's, she climbed the stairs, determination written all over her face.

The teacher had been well apprised of Ariane's situation and used a creative and unusual way to involve the little girl in the class activities. So engrossed did Ariane become that half an hour later, when Donovan tapped her on the shoulder to tell her he'd see her later, she simply fluttered her fingers and went back to work assembling the puzzle she'd been given, although she did spare a big smile for Abby.

"You owe me a double butter pecan." Abby brushed a hand against the glossy dark hair, then followed Donovan from the room and to the car.

"That went well. Where did you learn to deal with little girls?" he asked as he pulled out of the parking lot. He made it sound as if she inhabited Mars where children weren't allowed.

"I was one, remember?" Abby frowned. "I had second thoughts about the first day of school, too."

"What did your parents do to reassure you?"

"Told me about all the lovely science courses I could take." She deadpanned a look at him. "I chose the painting corner."

"Were you good at painting?"

"Better at getting paint all over myself. Not a good thing."

He chuckled at the image she'd created. Silence stretched until her nerves screamed a protest. She had to break it.

"How's your work going?"

"It's different than I expected." Donovan frowned for a minute. "Everyone is so used to the agency's way of handling our PR that trying to spring new ideas is hard work. But I'll get there."

"I'm sure you will. What kind of ideas?"

His face altered as if he hesitated to say what was really on his mind.

"Donovan?" Her stomach clenched. Something was up.

"Grandmother is supposed to be the one to tell you this, but I'm guessing she hasn't gotten around to it yet."

"To what?" Her forehead pleated in a frown. "What's wrong?"

"Nothing's wrong. She just wants us to work together and come up with a new image for the jewelry department at Woodwards." He held his breath, hoping Abby wouldn't flatly decline.

"Work together? Us?" She frowned. "I don't know anything about marketing."

"But you know a lot about the jewelry department."

"True." Abby had been itching to make changes for ages although there'd been no opportunity to do much with Winifred out sick. "But I'm up to my ears right now. Especially with the contest. I can't fit another thing into the day."

"It doesn't have to take a lot of your time. Maybe you could tell me what you envision and I could come up with something. I've already done a survey of our client base. Age, income, all those variables that go into a wedding. I needed the info for the national campaign I'm supposed to get rolling."

"I see." This sounded like it would entail a lot of contact with Donovan, something Abby wanted to avoid.

"The thing is," he paused to turn a corner. "In all our departments, we miss a large demographic. People think of us only as a bridal store or as wedding planners."

"And Woodwards has more to offer than that." She nodded, intrigued in spite of herself. "It's true of jewelry, too. Who would you target first?"

"Middle-aged to seniors, baby boomers, folks with disposable income who want to celebrate their past or look ahead to the future."

"Actually, the ring I'm working on now is for someone in exactly that group." Abby wasn't sure how much to tell him and whatever she did say had to be held in strictest confidence.

"Senior or baby boomer?"

"Senior. He's a wealthy man who has spent his life making money and now he realizes that the only joy it brings is in sharing it with someone he really cares about. That's what I want to show in my ring." She huffed a sigh of frustration. "That's what I thought I was showing until Ariane drew that gardenia."

"Grandmother loves gardenias," Donovan murmured.

Abby remained silent. He pulled into the parking lot, parked the car and studied her.

"You already knew that."

"Yes." She couldn't bring herself to break a confidence.

"She's a senior. So is Art. He definitely has a lot of money. Look at his car."

Abby looked at Donovan instead. Saw understanding dawn.

"You're saying Art is going to give my grandmother a diamond ring?"

"I'm not saying anything at all."

"You don't have to." Donovan laid one arm on the steering wheel, his shock obvious. "But—they've just met!"

"Correction. *You* just met him. Winifred has known him for quite a while in very intense circumstances. That makes a difference."

"Does the family know?"

"Of course not. This is Art's secret. He wants to do it his way. I have no intention of spoiling that." She gathered her purse, undid her seatbelt. "And neither can you," she warned, glaring at him.

"But—marriage?" Donovan gaped. "She's been a widow for—"

"Too long. Art makes her happy." Abby avoided his stare. "Anyway, no one said anything about marriage to me. I was commissioned to make a gift and that's what I'm doing."

"Come on. A ring with a three-carat diamond?"

"Would be a very nice gift. It doesn't have to automatically mean marriage." She climbed out of his car and shut the door, suddenly irritated by his comments. "But what if it does? Surely that's up to them to decide? Why should you object, except that you'll have to find your own place to live?"

His mouth opened and closed, but no sound came out.

"Isn't this exactly what we've been talking about? Figuring out the needs and wants of those who could be Woodwards' new clients?"

Abby studied him for a moment, then walked swiftly into Woodwards. She went directly to her office and dealt with each and every matter that came up. At five o'clock she shut her door, pulled out Ariane's sketch and went to work, forming a delicate but strong platinum gardenia that would shelter but also enhance the dazzling diamond she'd chosen. By nine-thirty Abby had a prototype that amazed even her. She dialed a number.

"Are you busy?"

"You have something?"

"A preliminary."

"I'll be right there."

Ten minutes later, Art buzzed the back door.

"I hope you like it," Abby murmured as she led him to her office. She slid a cloth off her work and showed him.

His reaction was everything she could have wanted.

"God surely does know how to direct a fellow to the right person for the job. And he certainly gave you a talent, Abby." He bent, studied the ring from every angle.

Abby waited, nerves on tenterhooks.

This wasn't God's doing, she wanted to yell. *This is me in spite of God.* God hadn't been part of her life since Donovan walked out on her and their dream. At least, she'd thought it was theirs.

"Finish it." Art straightened, pulled out his checkbook and wrote in a sum that made her eyes pop. "This is your commission. Use it however you want."

"Thank you," she whispered. "Thank you very much."

"Don't thank me, Abby." He tilted on his heels, his face shadowed. "God has blessed you with a glorious gift that deserves to be displayed. But can I give you some advice?"

"Of course." She held herself very still, waiting for the changes she was certain he'd ask for.

"There are a couple of verses in the Bible—I think I was meant to pass them on to you."

"I see." Why didn't God give her the verses himself?

Art pulled a piece of paper from the stack on her printer and began writing in a big, ranging scrawl.

Don't copy the behavior and customs of this world, but be a new and different person with a freshness in all you do and think—Matt 10:29–31.

"That's the NCV translation," he added as he handed the paper to her.

A freshness in all you do and think. So God approved the contest?

"Thank you." Abby stuffed the paper into a pocket. "Art, you realize you won't be able to give this ring to Winifred if I enter it in the contest?" She had to be certain he understood he couldn't pop it on her finger right away.

"Time's not right for us yet," Art agreed quietly. "But it is right for you. Get that thing finished and on the way to New York. Then get started on the next one."

"Any ideas what that should be?" Abby tossed him a cheeky grin.

Art didn't laugh. Instead his demeanor grew quite serious.

"You're going to the wrong source. I'm not the one you should be asking."

She knew he meant God.

Abby thanked him again for his generous check, but after Art had left and she stood alone in the massive Weddings by Woodwards building, she couldn't stop his words from repeating inside her mind.

Could it really be that for five years she'd misunderstood God? That he didn't want to foil her goals but to help her achieve them? That God had actually given her the need to create jewelry?

No. If that were true, then God would have given her parents who understood her dreams, who encouraged her to reach for them and achieve them. He would have kept Donovan here so he could support her dreams.

For so long Abby had been fighting to achieve her goals. Surely God should have eased her path, helped her.

Shouldn't he?

For a tiny infinitesimal moment Abby wondered what Donovan would say about it. But then she recalled the verse. *New and different; freshness in all you do and think.*

Definitely time to get rid of the old pattern of worrying about what other people would think and be who she really was.

"Grandmother, there's no need to explain. If you don't like the idea, I'll come up with another. It's not a problem."

But it was. More than two weeks and so far nothing Donovan had been able to suggest seemed to jibe with Winifred's ideas. Neither was he making much headway with Ari. She still held herself at a distance from everyone, including him. Donovan was frustrated.

"I appreciate the work you've put into this, son. It's just— not quite there yet."

"So I'll pull together some different ideas tomorrow. Right now I think I'd better go in search of Ariane. She's been waiting quite a while."

"You haven't found a place for her to spend afterschool hours yet?" Winifred's disapproval was obvious. "It's not good for her to be alone so much, Donovan."

"I know. Olivia thinks she's got a place locked down in the daycare she and Reese use when they have to work late, but the spot isn't available until the first of the month. Until then, I don't have any other choice but to have Ari brought here."

"I would have thought there would be some afterschool programs she could join in, but at least she'll soon be with other children. She needs to open up." Winifred closed the portfolio he'd given her and handed it back. "Talk to Abby again and let me know as soon as you have something else I can look at."

"Will do, Grandmother." Donovan bent, kissed Winifred's white curls and left her office pretending nonchalance.

The truth was he was fresh out of ideas, and for an idea man that was unacceptable. Worse than that, he did not want to keep running to Abby. She'd told him the changes she envisioned. That should be enough.

Only it wasn't. He couldn't seem to translate those ideas onto paper.

"Hey, Katie, have you seen Ariane? I know she arrived, but—"

"The driver dropped her off a while ago. She was in here for a bit, but then she left. Maybe to get a drink? I wasn't paying attention. Sorry." Katie offered him a distracted look as she hurried away to solve some problem.

Fiona ushered a client out of a fitting room and through the front door before dragging a hand through her hair.

"That was a toughie. She has no clue what she wants."

"Those are your best weddings, Mom," he cheered her on with a hug. "Seen Ariane?"

"Olivia was here with her and the twins when I went in for the consult. Olivia wouldn't have just left her alone. She may have wandered off somewhere. In my experience, girls usually like the fabric room." Fiona glanced at her watch, smiled at the woman entering the building. "Hello. I'm so glad you made it."

Fiona gave him a questioning look.

"Go on with your client. I'll find her," he whispered.

"Thanks, honey. We have to check out that reception hall tonight or I'd—"

Donovan shook his head at her and pointed. "Go."

The rest of the family was equally involved in business, so Donovan didn't bother them, simply walked through the enormous building, intentionally leaving Abby's section until last. Not that he was avoiding her, exactly.

Okay, he was. But fatherhood meant he was supposed to handle whatever problems came up, not depend on someone else to solve them. Donovan couldn't help glancing toward the jewelry designer's domain. When he saw a small dark head next to Abby's toffee-toned one, he realized he'd have to face Abby sooner than he'd planned. He moved to the doorway to watch.

"I really like the way you've made that banding line accentuate the front of the bracelet, Ariane," Abby murmured. "It looks a lot neater now."

Ari smiled to herself as she threaded another bead onto a pliable string that already held a number of beads. She worked quickly, threading, twisting, tying, until she caught sight of him in the doorway. Immediately she set down her things and walked over to him as if duty called.

"Hey, Ari. Had a good day?" He watched as she demonstrated what she'd done today. After a moment, she got around to showing him a bracelet. "Christmas?" he guessed. "You're making a Christmas present?"

She nodded, happily adding another few beads.

"Wow!" Donovan tried to pay attention as she demonstrated her ideas for several other gifts, then grinned at Abby. "Your influence, I presume. Still figuring out your Christmas gifts six months ahead of time, I see."

"Six? That's leaving it a bit late, isn't it?" She motioned for Ari to put away the bead kit. "I hope you don't mind that she came here. We've been working together for the past couple of days. She's a natural."

"I should pay you for watching her."

Abby's pretty face flushed and Donovan realized how wrong that sounded.

"I meant to say, it's very kind of you to watch her when you've got your own work to do. I'm hoping to get her into daycare within the next couple of weeks, so I'll try not to let her trouble you again."

"Daycare, huh? Well, at least she'll meet some more kids. She was telling me about a girl named Jessica today. They seem to be growing pretty close."

Jessica? Donovan was certain he'd never heard the name before. When he glanced at Ari he saw she was deliberately not looking at him. How had Abby, who supposedly detested kids, managed to figure that out?

"Maybe you could arrange a play date for them or something." Abby studied him, her brown eyes clear, transparent. "Or I could take them for ice cream. Ariane still owes me one large butter pecan."

"I don't think so. But thanks anyway." Donovan felt churlish saying it, but getting close to Ari was proving much harder than he'd imagined. Judging by what he'd just seen, Abby was light years ahead of him in that department and it stung. "I think we can manage."

"Of course." Abby bent, picked up a tiny plastic suitcase. "This is a little bead kit I put together for Ariane so she can work at home. She said her dolls haven't arrived from overseas yet. At least," a furrow of confusion wiggled across her forehead. "I think that's what she was trying to say."

"Some of our stuff has been slow." He ignored the suitcase. "But Abby, you don't have to go to all this work. Ari and I are fine. Grandmother's great company."

"Yes. Art told me you spend a lot of time together."

She held his gaze with a steadiness that forced Donovan to look away because he knew he'd been using his grandmother to buffer the strangeness between him and Ari.

"A friend of mine leads a Girl Guide troop not far from Winifred's house. They're really into beading," Abby murmured. "And I know of a Saturday morning puppet club that Ariane might—"

"No!" Both females startled, gaped at him. Donovan swallowed. "Sorry. Thanks anyway, Abby. It's just that I don't want to start Ari in anything until things are a little more settled. I'll get around to it, but I have to take my own time."

Abby's face drained of all color.

"I was only trying to help. Sorry I interfered. I won't do it again." She turned away to tidy her desk.

"I showed Grandmother my preliminary work on your department updating. She'd like us to try again. When would you be free to talk about it?"

"You'll have to set a time. Let me know and I'll try to be there." Abby kept her back turned. Her voice was icy.

A moment later the phone rang. Abby rushed away to see a client, but not until she'd hugged Ariane and given her the little suitcase.

For him, Donovan noted, Abby didn't offer even the smallest smile.

Ariane frowned at him.

"I know. I blew it," he muttered as he trailed behind her out of the room. "I seem to do that a lot lately." Ari ignored him.

He prayed for inspiration all the way home, but even God seemed silent.

Chapter Five

"**I**'m sorry, Grandmother. I can't make it."

"I beg your pardon?" Winifred rose from the dining room table and stretched to her tiny height, her eyes glacial. "You will be there, Donovan. You must be there. I specifically called the heads of the various departments together for this meeting tonight. That includes you."

"I can't get a sitter." He blinked when Winifred tapped her tiny fist on the table. "I did send you an e-mail mentioning that tomorrow morning might be a better choice."

"Tomorrow morning is *not* better for me." His grandmother shared a look with Art who excused himself from the table and took Ariane with him. "This is not working, Donovan."

"I really am sorry, Grandmother. As soon as I get things settled—"

"That's exactly the problem. You're not getting things settled."

The weight of the past weeks' lack of success, combined with her obvious dissatisfaction preyed on Donovan. But what could he do? He was only one man with too many calls on his time.

"I'm trying, Grandmother."

"No. What you're doing is juggling, trying to be all things to all people." Winifred moved to sit beside him. "I know you feel a great responsibility for Ariane. And I know how badly you want to make up for lost time and take your place in the company."

"You don't think I should have come home?" He'd never even considered that he might be putting a spike in Winifred's plans, instead of helping out.

"Of course you should have come home. And you do have to spend time with Ariane. But you don't have to do either all alone."

"I don't know what you mean."

"Don't you?" Those eagle eyes pierced through his protestations. "Then I'll speak plainly. Ariane needs more than just you in her world."

"But she has school and church."

"Where you watch her constantly. You're trying too hard to protect her, Donovan. You want to keep her from being hurt again. That's understandable. But she needs the bumps and bruises of life to find her normality. Keeping her in this cotton-wool world where you are always in control isn't healthy."

"Is that what I'm doing?"

"Isn't it?" Winifred touched his shoulder. "Kids love to explore. But Ariane shrinks back from that. She won't go out in the garden unless you're nearby. She doesn't laugh and giggle and romp like Reese's twins."

"You think that's because I'm too overbearing?" It hurt to hear this when he'd tried his hardest to help the little girl.

"You want her to forget, Donovan, and she'd like to please you, but she can't forget her past or her father." Winifred smiled. "Take it from a very old lady that the only way to get past pain is to work through it, not avoid it."

"So what do I do? Abandon her?"

"You always were a man of extremes," she said with a sigh. "Not abandon. Just set up her world so she's forced, little by little, to deal with it. That means putting her in someone else's care when sometimes you'd rather be there." She rose. "It won't be easy. You're going to have to depend on other people more and let them reach Ariane in their own way. But I think in the end, you'll both be happier for it."

Winifred began clearing the table. Donovan helped, man-handling a huge tray with her best china on it into the kitchen. A few moments later, Art appeared and he and Winifred began stacking the dishwasher as if they'd done it for years.

It was easy for Donovan to see he was in the way here. "I'll work on it, Grandmother."

"Good. In the meantime, the meeting starts in forty minutes. Abby gave Ariane that bead kit. Maybe she can work on it while the rest of us talk."

Donovan left the kitchen musing on what she'd said. The whole family would be there. That meant he couldn't ask his sisters or his brother to watch Ariane. She'd have to come along.

Abby would be there, too.

Her ability to relate so well to his goddaughter still bugged him. Donovan knew Ariane had been in Abby's office at least twice in the past week, but he also knew Abby had encouraged Ari to leave. Maybe because she was busy with her new project, maybe because she didn't like kids, although he now doubted that. Mostly, Donovan was certain, it was because he'd made it clear he didn't want Abby's interference.

Which wasn't exactly what he'd meant when he'd blurted out his comments. It was more a case of wariness. He didn't want Abby getting too close for two reasons. One, because Ari was his responsibility and he refused to shirk it. And two, he was afraid Abby would get too close to Ari and when Abby left for New York to fulfill her dream, Ari would feel abandoned.

Because Abby would be leaving. It was just a matter of time.

A tug on his pant leg forced Donovan to look down.

Ari held out the bead bag she'd been given.

"Do you mind working on it during our meeting? You'll have to be quiet." As if she was ever anything else. "You could lie down on the little couch in my office if you get tired."

Ariane nodded but didn't say anything. Donovan sighed. She looked so delicate, fragile. As if a bit of wind would knock her over. Why was Grandmother so certain she was strong?

"Let's go then. I'll try not to keep you up too late."

Ariane stared up at him, eyes expanding with excitement as she mouthed the word *Abby?*

"Yes, I'm sure she'll be there," he said as he walked beside her out to the car. "But she'll be part of the meeting, so she won't be able to talk to you."

The flare of interest died away. At Woodwards, Ari plodded beside him into the building. She sat exactly where he told her to. Even though she unfolded the case, she made no attempt to work with the beads.

Abby arrived just before Winifred called the meeting to order. Donovan saw her and Ari exchange a silent glance. He also noticed a tiny smile curve Ari's lips and the way she immediately dived into her beadwork.

"I've called this meeting to tell you all that I will be going to Chicago tomorrow and will remain there for the next several weeks. I want to make sure the new store is operating as I'd hoped. If there are difficulties, you each know who to contact, but I'm quite sure that there won't be any problems. You've managed without me for six months. A few weeks more should be simple."

She went over her plans for the next quarter, dealt with questions and cleared up whatever outstanding business was brought to her attention. When the meeting was adjourned, Reese cornered Donovan to point out some legal issues with an in-store contest he was thinking of running.

From the corner of his eye, Donovan watched Ariane beckon Abby over to admire her new work. The two seemed to share some kind of unspoken empathy that Donovan was at his wit's end to achieve. Ari didn't speak, yet Abby understood her gestures.

Shouldn't it be he with whom Ari had that bond?

"Are you listening to me, Don?" Reese followed his gaze. "Maybe Abby wouldn't mind staying with Ariane for a minute while I show you what I mean. I have it laid out in my office."

Of course he said it loud enough that Abby couldn't help but overhear. And naturally she agreed to stay with Ari. Donovan could hardly object, but he did his best to ensure that the discussion didn't take long.

Even so, the halls were deserted by the time he made his way back to the conference room. Only the low hum of Abby's voice carried to him.

"I know it's hard, sweetie. You miss your dad and your friends. But you have to try to make new friends." A little pause. "Of course it's not easy. When I was your age my parents insisted I had to be home every afternoon right after school. I don't know why because they weren't there. I was all alone in the house except for the housekeeper. I wanted so badly to go to Bridget's house, like the other girls on my block did, but my mom wouldn't allow it."

Donovan could imagine controlling Mary Franklin would have been threatened by the competition from another mother. He shifted so he could see into the room. Both Ariane and Abby were in profile.

"Bridget was the popular girl. Her mom was at home all the time. She made cookies and figured out games and was always laughing. All the kids had a great time at Bridget's house." Abby's voice drooped reflecting her sadness. "I wanted to be part of that, to learn how to play baseball and jump rope with them. But my parents didn't think that would be good for me. Instead they gave me books to read."

Ari made a motion with her hands that had Abby giggling.

"Yes, very boring books. I really tried to finish them, but after a while I started making up my own games."

So that's why Abby seemed to understand Ariane so well. She'd experienced some of the loneliness Ari was going through.

"No, I never really had many friends until I started fifth grade. That's when I met Donovan." Abby fell silent as if she was remembering.

Shaken by the wistful tone of her voice, Donovan stepped into the room.

"Sorry that took so long. Thanks for staying with her, Abby." He took a deep breath and did what he should have done days ago. "Actually, I'm really glad you did because I wanted to ask you about your friend's Girl Guide program. I think Ari might enjoy it. Can you give me a number to call?"

Abby looked at him as if he'd grown two heads, but obediently recited a phone number from memory. Ari also stared at him, but with a look of fear.

"Thanks. I'll check into it. And about that ice-cream cone we owe you."

"Don't worry about it." Abby gathered up her notes and rose. "It was just a game."

"Not at all. You won fair and square. Right, Ari?"

Ari, obviously confused, glanced back and forth between them.

"So it's up to you to collect. If you can tell me when you want to go, I'll make sure Ari has enough money."

"You're sure?" Abby paused, frowned, then nodded. "Yes, all right. I'd like to have my ice cream tomorrow afternoon, please. After Ariane comes from school."

"Is that okay with you?" he asked Ari whose eager agreement wasn't very flattering to him. "Good. Tomorrow afternoon. You'll have her back when?"

"You're not coming?"

"I can't. I have a meeting. More new concept ideas."

"It's Friday tomorrow. I have dinner with my parents tomorrow evening. Ari will be back here in plenty of time before dinner."

"Great. So that's all arranged." He zipped up the beading case and held out his hand to Ari. "Thanks again for staying with her. I guess we'll see you tomorrow. Hopefully we can get together soon to work out some new ideas for your department. Grandmother is pretty eager to see some progress."

"Yes."

She stood there, reticent and withdrawn and for once Donovan wished she'd smile and laugh like the old days.

"Goodnight, Abby."

"Goodnight. See you tomorrow, Ariane."

He felt Abby studying his back as he walked away, but Donovan kept going, holding all thoughts at bay until Ariane was fast asleep and he could sit alone in the garden. He took refuge in the gazebo while God conducted a lightning display.

Grandmother was right, and Abby's words about her past had only emphasized that. Parents were supposed to enable their children to deal with life, not hide them from it. He'd been trying so hard to protect Ariane, he'd forgotten her needs.

"I don't know how to do this," he reminded his heavenly Father. "I'm also at a loss to know how to help Grandmother's company. But I'm not shirking my duties and I'm not pretending anymore. Show me how to help."

The panic that had latched on during dinner slowly abated as the heavens roared and flared. When at last he went inside, Donovan knew only one thing.

Far from detesting kids, Abigail Franklin had some kind of connection with Ariane that did them both good. He could no more keep them apart and deny Ari her friendship than he could stop thinking about the lonely girl who'd grown into a woman able to touch a silent child's heart.

But that woman was now a confusing mix he didn't understand. Beginning tomorrow he was going to start asking some pertinent questions, questions he should have asked five years ago.

Maybe the answers would help him deal with odd new feelings he had whenever he was around Abby.

* * *

"A friend of mine in the business offered to show me some of his best campaigns. I'll be gone a couple of hours, but I should be back well before you have to leave for your dinner with your parents." Donovan grinned. "Enjoy the butter pecan."

"We will." Abby watched him leave, a slew of questions chasing through her mind.

Number one on the list was why this abrupt change toward her.

Ariane tugged her sleeve. Finding that answer would have to wait.

"You and I, Miss Chocolate-Chip-Ice-Cream, are about to go on a taste test at my most favorite place. It's called Lotsa Licks."

Most days, Abby studiously avoided the nearby old-fashioned ice-cream parlor for the sake of her hips. But today, with Ari's hand in hers, she headed straight for it. The place was hopping, as usual, and hardly any of the chrome and pink bar stools perched around glossy black tables were empty. But that didn't matter because what Abby had in mind was a taste test.

Tiffany Brick waggled a hand and waited for their approach.

"Hey, Abby. Haven't seen you in a while."

"After today you might not for a year. It took forever to work off the last cone you gave me."

"Still stuck on butter pecan?" Tiffany chuckled.

"Of course. But today my friend Ari is going to need to taste a whole bunch of flavors," she explained. "Just tiny tastes. Ari thinks chocolate chip is the only kind of ice cream for her. I'm aiming to change her mind."

"Then you're in the right place. Hold on a minute. I'll make up a sampler." Tiffany's samplers consisted of tiny quarter-teaspoons of different ice creams dotted over a foam plate. Since Lotsa Licks featured more than eighty-nine flavors, Tiffany had a lot of options.

Ariane's eyes grew huge as Tiffany assembled the tastes.

"There you go, honey. I've chosen twenty. Now you try those and see which one is your favorite."

"Thanks, Tiffany." Abby found them a seat and stocked up on napkins as Ariane began her taste test. "If you don't like one, leave it and taste another one," she advised when Ariane wrinkled her nose at the rum and raisin.

Watching the little girl was so much fun. Ariane didn't mask or hide her reactions. She stuck out her tongue or closed her eyes or smacked her lips. And through it all they giggled and laughed and enjoyed each other without saying a single word.

"I'm guessing that's your favorite," Abby murmured when Ariane returned to the bright pink ice cream and scraped the last droplet. "Shall we go order a cone of that kind?"

Ariane nodded eagerly, but she didn't rush up to the counter as another child might have. She waited until Abby rose and then carefully slid her tiny hand inside Abby's, a sweet smile lifting her lips. Abby's heart squeezed a bit tighter. Such a precious child. And she was missing so much because she couldn't or wouldn't talk.

"One cone of the pale pink stuff, please, Tiffany."

"Cotton candy. I'm not surprised. All the kids love it."

"I'll have a small butter pecan."

"You couldn't find a new favorite?" Tiffany teased.

"You almost got me with that mango chutney. Almost." Abby's cell phone rang. "Donovan? I can barely hear you."

"Accident. Be late. Ari." Static and noise cut through the transmission.

"I'll keep Ariane with me, don't worry. I'll take her to my parents if you're not back in time. Are you all right?"

"…okay. Fender…oil and the motor—"

The line went dead.

"Okay. I'll do that. Bye."

The pretense of a conversation was for Ari's benefit. Her face had gone completely white and her little hand trembled, almost dumping her ice cream.

"That was Donovan. His car broke down. He'll come as soon as he can. He said he's okay, Ariane." She prayed that was true.

It took some persuading but Ariane finally relaxed enough to finish most of her ice cream. Abby deliberately took the long way back to the store, ambling as if they had all the time in the world. But Donovan was not there.

Seeing the little girl's worry, Abby challenged her to a new beading pattern. But she couldn't stop herself from constantly checking the wall clock. Donovan's absence grew more worrisome when five-thirty arrived. She knew she could delay leaving no longer.

"Come on, honey. Let's put this stuff away. Then I'm going to take you to visit someone. Two someones." She smoothed over Ariane's worry, made a game of grocery shopping and singing silly songs as she drove to her parents' place.

The panicky look in Ariane's dark brown eyes intensified when Abby led her inside her parents' condo.

"Mom, Dad, this is Ariane, Donovan's goddaughter. Ariane, these are my parents, Mark and Mary."

"Hello, Ariane." Her mother watched Ari shake hands with her husband, then grabbed Abby's arm and dragged her and the groceries into the kitchen. "It's rude for her not to respond."

"She doesn't speak, Mom." Succinct didn't satisfy her mother's curiosity, so Abby gave her a précis of Ariane's history before returning to the foyer.

Ariane wasn't there.

Her father's low rumble emerged from the living room. Abby looked inside and found Ari seated beside her father, both heads bent over the coffee table. They were studying her beads. Mark Franklin seemed unbothered by the child's silence because for every question he asked, Ari answered with actions.

Abby studied them for a moment before walking over to press a kiss against her father's head.

"Hi, Daddy."

"Hello, dear. I'm so happy you brought your daughter to visit."

Abby was going to correct him but a shake of her mother's head and his obvious joy at choosing the beads Ariane strung on a wire changed her mind. He wouldn't remember in an hour anyway.

"Can you two be finished with your work by the time I make some fajitas?" Abby asked, watching Ariane's face. The little girl nodded solemnly. Her father didn't answer.

Abby returned to the kitchen.

"It hasn't been a good day for him," her mother complained. "I wish you'd come earlier. And why did you bring that child with you? Surely if she's Donovan's, he should be caring for her, not letting—"

"He was in an accident, Mom. He'll pick her up as soon as he can." Irritated that after five years her mother still couldn't cut Donovan any slack, Abby took it out on the onions and bell peppers.

Fridays were lean eating days at the condo. Her mother hated cooking and she used Abby's visit as an excuse not to. A bowl of cereal for breakfast and half a sandwich for lunch was what she called "saving up for Abby's dinner."

"Fajitas?" Her mother wrinkled her face in disapproval. "I'll have to be careful then. That greasy, spicy food never sits well with me."

Abby bit her tongue at the sour words and kept working. She fixed a nourishing green salad, prepared some crisp asparagus for steaming and arranged a fresh fruit salad, adding lemon cookies for dessert.

Still Donovan did not call.

Ariane was a delightful guest and her earlier tension dissipated as she showed Mark how to bead—until the doorbell rang and her mother escorted Donovan into the room. Ari jumped up but didn't move, her big eyes filled with trepidation.

"Your little girl was quite upset," Mary snapped at him.

"I'm sorry." Donovan walked over and swung Ari into his arms, hugging her. "Okay?" he asked softly.

Although Ari held back, she nodded at him, her little body relaxing. Donovan held her for a few minutes longer before whispering something when she touched a bruise on his forehead.

As she watched, Abby's heart pinched. Five years ago she'd daydreamed about Donovan holding their child. But she'd never imagined this. The way he held Ari, the look of love in his eyes—it was clear this child occupied his heart.

"It's okay," he murmured as Ari brushed away a spot of dirt on his cheek. "I'm fine. But the car's a mess. You'll have to help me pick out a new one."

"Excuse me." Mary made a big deal of trying to squeeze past him.

"I'm sorry to burst in and ruin your dinner, Mrs. Franklin."

Abby took one look at her mother's face and jumped in.

"You didn't ruin anything, Donovan. We haven't started yet and there's plenty to share. Join us."

"I'm not sure—"

For once Abby's father seemed perfectly normal as he insisted Donovan stay.

"But I hope you don't eat as much as you used to," Mark teased, his tired eyes winking with fun. "Abby's fajitas are my favorite and I'm starving."

"I remember them well, sir." Donovan shared a glance with Abby, reminding her of how often he'd stayed for meals she'd made. "I promise only that I'll try to leave you a few scraps."

"I suppose I should be grateful," Mark joked as he shook Donovan's hand and drew him toward the table where Abby quickly set another place.

"I tried to call, but your cell isn't working, Abby." Donovan leaned toward her, his voice soft. "Because your parents are unlisted, I had to get Reese to check the company records to find this address."

"Not working?" Abby checked her phone. "It's dead," she muttered, embarrassed.

"That explains it then." Donovan glanced at Ariane who was indicating they should all fold their hands for the saying of grace.

Abby's embarrassment grew. Her parents weren't faith kind of people—

"God, we thank you for this meal our daughter has prepared and we ask you to bless it to us. In your name, Amen," Mary said.

"Amen," Mark repeated.

Abby blinked. Her mother was saying grace? Since when?

"So Donovan, did you find what you needed in Europe?" Mary asked.

It came out sounding caustic. Abby rushed to intervene. "Mom, it's not—"

"I learned a lot of things I needed to learn," Donovan responded evenly, his features unruffled.

"I always wanted to tour Europe, especially Paris. But of course in our day, money was tight and we had to save for college."

"I hope one day you'll go." Donovan served Ariane salad. "After all, you're free now. You don't have to worry about Abby. You can live your own dream. Dreams are the one thing none of us can or should give up."

Her mother and Donovan exchanged a look that held a boatload of meaning that Abby couldn't decipher. She sensed animosity between the two and figured he'd deliberately used the word "dream" to goad her mother. But Abby had never been able to arbitrate between them.

And tonight she didn't want to. Let them settle old scores themselves.

For a few minutes the meal continued in silence. But then Mark asked about Donovan's work and a fragile peace was restored. By the end of the meal Mary was even discussing taking a French language class.

"Please let me help with the dishes," Donovan said when Abby rose to clear the table.

A tinkle from the piano in the other room drew her mother's frown and Mary scurried away to make sure her beloved baby grand was safe. Mark followed.

"I used to be scared of them," Donovan admitted as he helped carry the dishes to the kitchen. "Your mother especially. She always seemed so strong. Maybe it's me, but tonight I don't see that."

"Really?" Abby handed him a scraper to clean the plates while she rinsed the pots.

"She seems tired, sad, almost as if she's given up. I suppose your father's condition takes its toll."

"That must be it." She was going to ask about the "dream" comment he'd made, but when the sound of "Chopsticks" echoed on the piano, Abby quickly moved to the doorway to see what was going on.

"Is something wrong?"

"That was never allowed when I was a child," she explained.

Donovan raised his eyebrows when, with patient tender concern, Mary repeatedly demonstrated the correct keys until Ariane picked up the melody. Soon the two of them were laughing as they hammered out the little song together, her father clapping merrily in the background.

Abby returned to the kitchen stunned, and truth to tell, a little upset.

"I'm sorry her being here bothers you." Donovan, shirt-sleeves rolled up, was scrubbing the skillet she'd used.

"Who?"

"Ari."

"It doesn't bother me that she's here." She stacked the last glass in the dishwasher and started it. "I'm glad she and my mom are able to relate to each other."

"Really?" He looked unconvinced.

"Of course." Faint wistful sounds of a new melody carried through the rooms. Abby recognized it as one of the first songs her mother had tried to teach her. "Do you think I begrudge my parents a little companionship?"

"No. But I remember your telling me how clumsy and awkward you felt when your mother made you practice your piano lessons. I remember how upset you always got. And," he added quietly, "I saw your face just now when you looked at your mother bent over Ari. It can't be easy to watch her fawn over another child when your relationship was so difficult."

In fact, it was extraordinarily painful. Why couldn't her mother have used those soft dulcet tones with her? Why couldn't she have sat beside her on the piano bench and encouraged Abby the way she was encouraging Ariane? Why did everything between them have to be a contest of wills?

Donovan touched her shoulder.

"I'm sorry, Abby."

"Don't be sorry," she said, easing away from him. "Look at them, both of them. Dad's having a great time poking through those beads. And Mom's in her element with such a responsive student. For a little while, they're happy."

She turned away, unable to watch any more. Her heart ached with questions.

Like why hadn't *she* ever made them that happy?

Abby braced herself and pulled open a drawer to find a clean dish towel. A Bible lay inside, open to *Romans*. Passages had been underlined in red, dated. Her mother not only said grace but now read the Bible?

"I'm going to have to beg a ride home for us, Abby." Donovan dried the last pot. "I took a cab over."

"What exactly happened?"

"A guy had a heart attack, lost control of his vehicle and hit me. Fortunately, I wasn't going very fast, but it was still a hard impact and my car got mashed against the side rail."

"You weren't hurt?"

"Amazingly enough not. And the EMS people were able to revive the man. Still, I'm very glad Ari wasn't with me. She doesn't need another accident. She was there when George died and she hasn't come fully to grips with that yet."

"I think she sensed all wasn't well. You'll probably have to do some reassuring tonight."

"How'd the ice-cream thing go?"

"Cotton candy is the new fave."

They were talking, making conversation, but saying nothing important.

"Are you two ever going to finish those dishes?" her mother called.

Abby guessed Donovan had no real desire to spend a Friday evening with her parents, but because he'd eaten with them, he probably felt he had to stay a short time. Knowing her mother and Donovan were like oil and water, Abby was actually dreading the next few minutes and fully expected that after a decent time had elapsed, he'd make an excuse, call a cab and leave.

But she was proven wrong when Donovan spotted her father's Chinese checkers game on a side table and challenged Mark to a game. Ariane also wanted to play. Abby thought that's why her mother gracefully agreed to join in. Two hours later her father had beaten them all twice and her mother insisted they needed more nourishment.

"How about milk and cookies?"

About to decline, Abby caught the wistful look on Mary's face as she stared at Ari. The child was begging Donovan to stay. He finally gave in, though reluctantly.

"Where did the girl get those bead things from?" her father asked her while the others set out the snack.

"From me. She stopped by my office one day and started fiddling, so I got her a kit."

"Do you think you could get me one?"

"Are *you* going to design jewelry, Dad?" The rude comment slipped out without thinking. Abby's face burned in shame and she opened her mouth to apologize.

"Why should you have all the fun? I might have tried it years ago if I'd known how interesting it is." He winked at her. "Are they expensive?"

"Of course not. I'll bring you some next time I come. Okay?"

"Thanks, Abby. Only, could you find bigger beads? Those dinky things make me all thumbs. I like to get a grip on what I'm working on." He flexed his fingers.

"I have a better idea. Why don't you and I go shopping for some supplies tomorrow?" She was supposed to be working on her entries for the contest tomorrow. But the beading gave her father such joy. "You can choose exactly what you want."

"That's a fine idea," he crowed as he rose to heed his wife's call to the table. "I'm going to practice a bit before I try actually making something."

Since Ariane was visibly drooping by the time they finished the cookies, Abby felt no compunction about leaving. But as they walked out of the condo toward her car, a flicker of uneasiness trembled in her midsection at the prospect of twenty minutes alone with Donovan. Avoiding him wasn't working out very well.

She waited while he belted Ariane into the backseat, then climbed in himself.

"It was a nice evening. Thanks for sharing with us, Abby. And for jumping in when I couldn't be there. I appreciate it."

"My mother wouldn't admit it, but I think she and my father both enjoyed tonight." Abby remembered the Bible in the drawer, the quiet grace. "You said she seemed weary. Is that the only difference you noticed in my mother?"

"Funny you'd ask that." He frowned, rubbed his chin. "When I first got there, I thought same old, same old. But when she said grace, and later, when she seemed to mellow with Ari, I wondered if something had happened to change her."

"Like what?" Abby wanted him to elaborate without input from her.

"Like maybe she's begun soul-searching. She said grace in a personal way, as if she was talking to someone she knew and not simply reciting out of habit."

"And you think that means she's had some kind of conversion?" Abby scoffed, remembering her mother's sharp attitude when she'd arrived with Ariane.

"I can't say and I'd only be guessing anyway. But maybe she's begun to consider her faith. That's often how it starts—asking God questions."

"That's what you did?"

"Sort of. George's death came as a complete and unexpected shock. He was always there, my best friend and closest ally. I helped him with Ari from the time she was two. They were like my substitute family."

As the Woodwards had been hers, Abby reflected.

"But then George was gone and I was left in charge. My secure little world was upended and I didn't know anything for certain except that somewhere God was watching over me." He smiled at her. "Believe me, it was totally humbling to realize that I, the spin doctor who manipulated everything, couldn't spin this to make it palatable."

"I see." Abby chewed her bottom lip. "So you were able to deal with your situation by renewing your faith?" She didn't understand that.

"I *am* able to deal with it by realizing that God has the answers and by accepting that he will show me the way to go if I put my faith in him." Donovan's smile flashed in the dim glow from the dash. "That's the toughest part of it, you know. Putting my faith in someone other than myself."

"Explain that," Abby said as she turned down Winifred's street.

"I never really had goals." A rueful note edged his voice. "It was my way of avoiding conflict. Mr. Fun, skate through life, forget about the future and focus on today. Me, me, me. My way. That's how I got through life."

"And?"

"There's a reason God put us on this earth. It's not just to satisfy our wants," he said quietly. "God has to be the directing force in the choices we make or we're destined to make a lot of mistakes."

Abby pulled into the driveway and shifted into park. Ariane stirred in the backseat. There would be little time for more conversation and yet she needed to hear about his life in Europe.

"Can I ask you something, Abby?"

"I guess." She waited warily.

"Why didn't you ever use that scholarship and go to college?"

"Huh?" She stared at him blankly.

"I was told you won a full scholarship." He named a prestigious college. "I thought for sure you'd take it, given the college's proximity to New York."

"You must have misunderstood. There was no scholarship. Why would you think there was?"

"I heard—never mind." Donovan studied her for several minutes, as if he couldn't quite accept what she'd said. By then Ariane had completely awakened. He climbed out of the car and Abby's questions died unasked.

"Thanks a lot, Abby. We appreciate your help today." Donovan swung Ariane into his arms, closed the car door, then bent to murmur, "Goodnight."

"Goodnight."

As soon as they were inside, Abby drove away. But the trip home was anything but peaceful.

Why did everyone seem to be connected to God but her?

Chapter Six

Abby's presence at church on Sunday morning surprised Donovan so much that he didn't have a ready excuse when Ariane dragged him toward her.

"Hi." Abby looked as elegantly stylish as always in her dark linen dress. A delicate silver butterfly with multicolored wings was her only ornament.

"Hi, yourself." He bent to get a closer look at the pin. "Yours?" As if he had to ask.

"Test project for the contest. Do you like it?"

"It's gorgeous. You've been busy."

"Not as busy as I should be. I spent yesterday morning with Dad. Thanks to this little miss, he's taken up the hobby of beading. Your grandmother asked me to come and hear Art sing this morning. He has quite a voice." She chucked Ariane under the chin and smiled so wide Ari couldn't help but return it. "And you? Any more ideas for the jewelry revamp?"

"None. I seem to have lost all creativity. If I ever had any."

People were bumping them, trying to move past.

"We seem to be blocking traffic. Maybe we should step outside," Abby suggested when Fiona pointedly squeezed past.

Distracted by Ariane tugging on his sleeve, Donovan

followed Abby outside, ignoring his goddaughter's motions to invite Abby for lunch. When he glanced up, he realized Abby understood exactly what Ari wasn't saying. But she was pretending not to. And Donovan knew why. He'd brushed off Abby's attempts to help before and she wasn't going to offer again.

"Since there never seems to be any time to meet at work, maybe we should put our heads together today. Are you free for lunch? Ari and I usually pick up something and eat in the park if it's nice."

"I was going to work this afternoon." Gold flecks in her hazel eyes glittered.

"I have to, also. But we do need to eat." Donovan gave way to the tug inside and wheedled, "Grandmother's going to want something concrete from us soon."

"Okay."

Abby agreed to meet them near the pavilion at Cheesman Park. On the way there, Donovan remembered he was supposed to be avoiding her. Managing on his own. But wasn't that exactly what Grandmother had criticized? Besides, it was only lunch. He wasn't going to ask her to help with Ariane again.

Abby beat him to their meeting spot. She sat on a huge quilt, talking to a man who hurried away as soon as he caught sight of Donovan and Ariane.

"Friend of yours?" he asked curiously.

"Our old school chum, Billy Coombs." Abby giggled at his surprise. "I think he was a bit intimidated when he saw you."

"Intimidated? By me?" Donovan snorted. "I don't think so. He's got six inches and about fifty pounds on me."

"And a very good memory of your threat the night we graduated." Abby was trying to hide her smile and not succeeding.

"That was five years ago!"

"That was a big threat."

"I was eighteen. Give me a break." He sank down on the

blanket. "I was pretty mad when he asked you out, but I never intended to spray paint his car."

"Because he still drives it, I guess Billy isn't taking any chances." Abby's gaze fastened on the video game Ariane had pulled from her backpack. "New toy?"

"It's supposed to be educational," he defended, concentrating on unpacking the lunch he'd purchased.

"Donovan, she has six games here."

He sighed. Abby wore a frown that intensified when Ari showed her some of the other things he'd bought. She drew pictures of items she'd left at home.

"Lunchtime. Let's say grace." It wasn't his best effort at talking to God, but Abby's silence threw him off.

Conversation, already stilted, halted completely as they ate. Abby barely touched her pizza, even though he knew ham and pineapple was her favorite. Ari, oblivious to the tension, ate heartily, then motioned that she was going to try the nearby slide. Donovan nodded.

"What are you doing, Donovan?"

"Pardon?" He repackaged the chocolate cake Abby wouldn't touch. "I don't know what you mean?"

"Yes, you do. You went on a spending spree yesterday. Judging by these," she held up Ari's drawings, "a really big spending spree."

"I just bought a few things to make her more comfortable."

"A portable DVD player will make Ariane more comfortable?" she challenged. "A pile of new clothes and a stereo and a bunch of toys can do that?"

"Abby, you don't understand."

"Explain it to me."

He wanted to. He wanted her to understand how badly he needed not to fail at making this little girl feel at home in her new world.

"Well?" she pressed.

"I don't have the same rapport with her that you do," he blurted. "I want to, but somehow I just can't connect with her. I feel like she's always comparing me, and what I do, to George."

"She probably is," Abby agreed.

"Thanks. That helps." He shook his head.

"That is the only life experience Ariane has, Donovan. But comparing you doesn't mean she thinks you're doing anything wrong. It just means she finds it different."

"So different she cries herself to sleep at night," he muttered, shamed by the admission.

"If you honestly think clinging to a portable DVD player is going to comfort her, you've changed more than I imagined, Don."

The acerbic timbre of Abby's voice told him she was mad. One glimpse at her eyes and all doubt fled. The gold sparks blazed with anger.

"I don't know what to do for her, Abby."

"Yes, you do. You're just scared to do it."

That stung.

"Feel free to punch a guy when he's down."

"What I'd like to do is knock some sense into your head," Abby snapped. "When you heard her crying, what was your first instinct?"

"To run."

She lifted her eyebrows.

"It was," he insisted. "Then I thought maybe I should hold her or something."

"I'm no child expert, but that sounds like a good idea." She studied him. "So why not go with that impulse?"

Why had he even told her? It was none of Abby's business what he did or bought or how he dealt with Ariane.

Except that Abby truly cared about Ari.

"Why, Donovan?"

"She was whispering George's name, begging for him to take her with him." He shook his head. "I couldn't interrupt that."

"Why not?"

"I don't know."

"Then I'll tell you why. It's because you're afraid to build a deeper relationship with her. Because as long as she's quiet, docile, plays on the swing without asking you to push her," she said, pointing to Ari who was using one toe to propel herself backward and forward, "As long as she manages on her own, you don't have to invest yourself in her life."

"That's not fair." Abby wasn't the only one who was mad now. "I've done everything I can to make the transition easier. Grandmother said I was too overprotective."

"It's not a transition, Donovan," she grated, her eyes hard. "It's Ariane in a new, unfamiliar world, and she needs someone who will let her have her sad moments, share her memories of her dad and encourage her to live—as he would have wanted. You don't have to protect her from that, you have to share it."

All fine and well to say, but how did that work? Donovan wondered.

"Technically you're her father, Donovan. Act like it." Abby watched Ariane shrink back as another child approached her. "What are you so afraid of?" she demanded.

"Failing."

"Guess what, Charm Boy? We all fail. And most of us get back up, dust off and try again. It's called life."

"I didn't miss this snide side of you, Abby."

"You didn't miss me at all," she said, her eyes hard.

"That's not true." He had, at first.

"Doesn't matter. It's time someone told you the truth." She patted his cheek and smiled that totally Abby-smile that lit up her skin from beneath. "Come on, Donovan. Suck it up. Admit you were never good at dealing with other people's emotions. But you're going to have to learn or that little girl will suffer more."

"How do I do that, Abby? Sometimes I think Ari only stays with me because I'm all that's familiar." That admission cost him.

"Baloney. She loves you, but she's afraid to show it in case you go away, too. Invest yourself in getting to know her. Engage her in the things she loves and she'll respond."

He thought about it for two seconds. "You want me to take up ballet?"

Abby hooted with laughter which brought Ariane running. She glanced at each of them curiously before flopping down on the blanket beside Abby. A moment later her fingers slipped into Abby's. Donovan felt alone.

"Maybe you could try something easy first."

"Like what?" he demanded. If she had all the answers, then he wanted to hear them.

Abby considered him for several moments before she faced Ariane.

"Honey, Donovan was wondering if you wanted to have one of your school friends over for a visit. What do you think?"

Donovan watched the girl closely, saw her eyes flare wide with excitement before fear doused them. She shook her head.

Suddenly he had an idea.

"Actually, Ari, I wondered if you and a friend would like to go for ice cream with me. We could go to that place you liked so much. What do you think?" He held his breath, praying the child wouldn't turn him down. *Just a chance, that's all I need, a chance to prove I can be trusted.*

Ari took only a minute to think about it before she pointed at Abby.

"You want her to come, too?

Ariane nodded. Was that hope he saw tucked in the back of her eyes?

"Okay, you talk to your friend at school tomorrow about what day would be a good day. I'm thinking Abby and I could take an hour off on Wednesday afternoon."

"Anyone care about my opinion?" Abby shot him a glare. But when Ari turned to her, she smiled and nodded. "Wednesday's fine."

"Great." He grinned at Abby. "Thanks."

"You're welcome. Now, let's go over your ideas for my department. I have to get to work soon."

"We went over my ideas. You were supposed to come up with some new ones." Abby stared at him blankly, so Donovan threw out his best thoughts, but Abby challenged every one.

"It's not the image we want," she kept repeating.

"So what is?" he said, frustrated by his inability to impress her. "Tell me what you envision."

"I don't know if I can." Abby leaned back, thought about it. "Sleeker without being cold. Alluring but not overpowering. With a touch of romance. Does that wiggle any of your creative marketing buttons?"

"I'll have to think about it."

"If we could do something to make the jewelry department feel less sterile, more welcoming. Maybe stools that are chrome and comfy leather in front of the cases. Or lights that give more sparkle and shimmer than the ones we now have. And displays that don't have to run in straight lines, at right angles." Abby helped him pack away the leftover food, then rose, folded the quilt and smiled at Ariane. "It's time I got back to work." She hugged Ari. "I'll see you on Wednesday, okay, sweetie?"

"Maybe tomorrow morning we can talk this over again?" Donovan wanted to get this nailed down and finally prove to Winifred that his years overseas hadn't been wasted.

"Maybe." Abby nodded, then hurried away.

Ari agreed she wouldn't mind a few pushes on the swing, so Donovan devoted himself to that for a while. He thought about what Abby had said in regard to his relationship with Ariane. Although he didn't want to admit it, she was right. He had tried to stay on the sidelines.

As he drove home, Donovan wondered where Abby had gained her experience of a child's needs. She hadn't won a scholarship, she'd said. Maybe the other things he'd been told weren't true either. The thing was, he didn't want to ask Abby about something he'd been told five years ago. He should have asked then. Bringing it up now would make him look like an idiot. Facing her mother with it would probably only make matters worse since Abby and Mary's relationship had always been strained. He wanted to spare Abby more pain.

It was getting harder to keep Abby at arm's length. And considering how willing she was to help him unlock Ariane's silence, Donovan wasn't sure he wanted to.

So where did that leave him?

"It's perfect." Art twisted the finished ring to and fro, admiring the shimmer of morning sunlight off the diamond's facets. "The gardenia is absolutely stunning. At first I thought it might look a bit old-fashioned, but nobody could say that about this ring."

"I'm just sorry you can't give it to Winifred right away," Abby mused. "But I have to ship it by courier today if it's to get to New York in time to meet the entry date."

"It's too early for me to give this to her," Art said, as he had before.

Abby closed the ring case but remained silent, privately wondering what was wrong.

"Winifred needs time," he said, as if reading her thoughts. "She has a lot going on right now and I won't do anything to add to her stress."

"I've never known anyone so determined to achieve his goal."

"Look in the mirror," he teased. "What are your ideas for the rest of the contest?"

"Still thinking. Somehow your ring will be the start of it, but I need to have five items altogether, and I haven't figured out exactly how to do that yet. I'm beginning to wonder if entering was such a good idea."

"Hey, Abby, I was hoping—oh, sorry," Donovan apologized. "I didn't realize you were busy. I'll come back."

"No, you won't. You'll stay and persuade this woman that giving up on her contest is exactly the wrong career move." Art moved to the door. "Don't you dare give up," he said before a hasty exit.

"You're giving up on the contest? But why?" Donovan sat down in her client chair and frowned. "That's your preliminary entry, isn't it?"

Abby nodded and when he took the ring box she let him, watching as he opened it. Donovan's vivid blue irises expanded and he whistled.

"Wow! This is fantastic, Abby. The best I've ever seen you do." He closed the lid and handed back the box. "Why would you quit now?" he asked quietly.

"I'm not quitting," she assured him. "Just having a down moment. I'm having difficulty coming up with a series theme. Nothing seems large enough to encompass what I want to do."

"And that would make you give up?" He shook his head.

"I'm not giving up," she reiterated wishing she'd never said a word to Art. "It's the time thing. I can never seem to get enough of it. But I'm not giving up on moving to New York, so don't worry. What did you need?"

"A few minutes of your time." He grinned and Donovan the charmer was back in full daunting force. "I wondered if you'd like to look at some houses."

"Houses?" Abby packaged the ring and beeped Katie to ask that it be shipped with plenty of insurance. "Is that part of the new campaign for my department?"

"Maybe. We agreed that we had to cover several generations." He smiled like the proverbial cat with cream. "Grandmother will be back this weekend and I would like to have some progress to report. I thought if we looked at some houses, we might get some ideas about who we're trying to reach."

"And you'd have a head start on a search for your new home."

"Two birds with one stone," he agreed.

"You're kidding, right? That's a pretty weak reason to skip work." She laughed. "It doesn't even make sense."

But it was tempting, so tempting, to be free for a few hours and ignore the pressure of coming up with a cohesive design that would win first prize and get her out of this town. Abby ached to say yes.

"Come on. You're not shirking your duties. It's part of the job."

"I can't, Donovan. I promised I'd take lunch to my parents. My mom hasn't been feeling well and Dad's a little more absent-minded than usual."

"I promise you'll have time for lunch with them," he said, grasping her hand and tugging. "But only if we leave right now."

Because he wouldn't listen to her excuses and she wanted to go anyway, Abby grabbed her purse and followed him from the building.

"I'm no marketer. Why do you need me?" she asked when he held open the car door.

"Because you'll know what's an appropriate look for the store." He closed her door with a triumphant grin and climbed into the driver's seat. "And maybe you can give me a hint about what Ariane will need in our new home. Girl things," he emphasized.

"Donovan, you have two sisters. Katie or Sara would be happy to help you find a home."

He made a big production of shuddering.

"They're not that bad."

"Katie would keep a list of good and bad features of the house, the mortgage, the school district, etcetera. And then she'd decide on the most appropriate house no matter what I thought about it. Sara, well, Sara, bless her heart, would pick the one most suited to her, which undoubtedly would not suit me. Think rooms with white fluffy rabbits and Olympic-sized bathtubs."

Abby couldn't help laughing.

"The first house I've arranged to see is older but supposedly has a lot of character, or so the agent claims." He rolled his eyes. "I think character means redoing the plumbing and fixing the roof, but it might give us some perspective on generational stuff for the store's campaign."

Donovan pulled up in front of a beautiful Victorian three-story house that had gingerbread trim, a wraparound porch and a massive tract of land to go with it.

"Old-fashioned but very lovely," Abby mused as she got out of the car. "Jewelry-wise this is us now, but not many clients go for that style anymore."

"Very fairy tale-esque, isn't it? Not exactly me."

As the agent showed them through the many rooms, Abby had to agree. Donovan would not be comfortable here. They moved on to the next home he'd chosen to see.

"Oh, my." Abby couldn't think of anything else to say that wouldn't give away her absolute hatred of the ultra-modern structure. But she held her tongue because Donovan was obviously enamored. She hoped the inside might be different, but it wasn't.

"You hate it."

"Hate is a strong word," she said solemnly. "But completely accurate. It's not appropriate for Weddings by Woodwards either, because it will exclude too many people who don't like modern. This style would pigeonhole us."

"And as a home?" he asked.

"I can't see Ariane living here," she said, glancing around. "There's no grass in the backyard, for one thing. And no mess."

"Why do you need a mess?" he asked, tracing one finger over the gleaming stainless steel counter.

"Do you see anyplace to leave your sneakers? Can you imagine Ariane dreaming fairy tales in all this glass and steel?"

"I suppose you're right. It's just that it would translate into a gorgeous PR campaign. And it reminds me a lot of a new sports car." Donovan laughed at her groan. "Not into cars?"

"Onward."

And so it went, house after house, until Abby glanced at her watch.

"Donovan, it's quarter to twelve and I have to take lunch to my parents!"

"No problem." He turned into the lane leading to Weddings by Woodwards' parking lot.

"Oh. Thanks." So now she had to scrounge up something to eat for the parents, she realized. She opened her door.

"No, stay there. I'll be back in a jiffy." He scooted out of the car and across the lot in seconds. In less than five minutes he was back lugging a huge cooler.

"What's that?" she asked as he stowed it in the backseat.

"Lunch for four." He grinned. "You should come out of your office more often. Today is test day in the kitchen. For the Jenkins–Matthews wedding. I'm getting a second opinion on the fare."

That was Donovan. Resourceful, ingenious and lots of fun.

Mary Franklin wasn't as appreciative.

"You brought us lunch from Woodwards?" she asked, her tone disgusted as Donovan unloaded the cooler. "Why?"

"Our chef is concocting a new menu for a big society wedding. Have you read of the Jenkins–Matthews wedding, Mrs. Franklin?"

"Of course." Suitably impressed, she remained silent until he'd unwrapped dish after dish. "This is for their reception?"

"That's the plan. The chef wants an unbiased opinion. I hope you're hungry, Mr. Franklin."

"First time you ever arrived with food, Donovan," Mark teased. He gaped at the array of dishes. "Think there's enough for all of us?" he joked.

Her father was in fine form today, but even if he hadn't been, Donovan's banter and quick exchanges seemed to cheer him. Abby's mother, on the other hand, seemed on edge. She kept sneaking glances at Donovan as if she expected him to attack every word.

"Who's saying grace?" Donovan asked when they were all seated around the table.

"I am," Mary said.

Once again Abby listened as her mother prayed. Where had she learned to talk to God like that, as if He was a benevolent parent who cared about minute details of life?

"Thank you, Mrs. Franklin. That was lovely." Donovan passing around the dishes.

"It was nice of you to bring this."

Abby blinked in surprise as her mother's voice changed to something approaching friendliness toward the same man she'd once called shifty and a fly-by-night when he'd quit his third summer job to work at a kids' camp.

"My pleasure."

"I'm starved." Mark pulled the napkin into his lap and waited expectantly.

"First course, creamed asparagus soup." Donovan served them.

That was followed by shrimp salad, Cornish game hens smothered in a delightful cherry sauce accompanied by tiny white potatoes, pearl onions and peas. Abby was certain Donovan had to be very tired of her mother's endless questions about the ingredients.

"Donovan doesn't work in the kitchens, Mother."

"Well, I'm sure he knows the family recipes." Mary leaned back in her chair, eyes narrowed, face tight. "Tell your chef that I think his meal is excellent."

"I will." Donovan checked his watch and began repacking the cooler. "I'm sorry to leave you with the dirty dishes, but Abby insists she be back at work at one."

"Abby has always understood duty," Mary said, her gaze riveted on Donovan. She rose. "Mark and I will clean this up."

"Thank you." Donovan preceded her to the door.

"Perhaps next time you can bring Ariane," Mary murmured, the harsh lines around her eyes and mouth easing.

"She'd like that. She was impressed by your piano."

"I could give her lessons. I'm well qualified to teach."

Abby couldn't believe it when Donovan nodded.

"I'll talk to her about it and get back to you." He swung the cooler up to his shoulders and said goodbye.

"Bye, Mom, Dad." Abby hugged them both, then hurried to catch up to Donovan. "You're going to let my mother teach Ariane?"

"If Ari wants to learn."

"But you can't!"

"Why not?" He frowned, studying her for a moment before storing the cooler and climbing into the car. "They seemed to get along okay."

"That was a few minutes one evening. A lesson means she'd be there for half an hour. With my mother."

"You make it sound like torture."

Abby nodded, remembering. "It was."

"Ariane's not you, Abby. Your mom seems to really enjoy her. I think they'd both enjoy some time together." He made a face. "I know you're going to get mad at me, but is it possible that you're jealous?"

"What?" She stared at him in disbelief.

"I'm serious. I know the struggles you've had with your mother. You always tried so hard and she never seemed to accept you for what you were." He drew a breath and continued. "But Ariane's not you. And your mother seems to click with her. Besides, Olivia suggested that if Ariane had an outlet like music, it might help her."

"I am not jealous of Ariane," she said, enunciating very clearly.

But no sooner had she said the words than Abby realized it

wasn't true. She did resent Ariane for being able to arouse motherly feelings in Mary that Abby had never witnessed. Years of obedience, of quashing her own opinions and desires had never achieved the acceptance Ariane had been able to generate in a few hours.

She was jealous. It was embarrassing and painful to admit, but it was true.

"Now you've gone all silent." Donovan sighed. "I knew I shouldn't have asked you to come with me this morning. I should have stuck by my original plan to avoid you and—"

"Avoid me?" That hurt. Abby blinked away the tears and glared at him. "Why do you want to avoid me? Have I done something wrong?"

"Oh, boy." Donovan took one look at her face and pulled into a cul-de-sac where he shifted the car into park. "That didn't come out right, okay? What I meant was—"

"I think you said exactly what you meant." She folded her arms over her chest and ordered her eyes to stop watering.

"I didn't say all of what I meant, okay, Abby?" Donovan waited a minute and when she wouldn't look at him, he tucked the tip of his forefinger under her chin and coaxed her head to turn. "Listen?"

She thought about it for a moment, then nodded. Once.

"I decided on the plane ride home that I would apologize for acting the way I did five years ago and then avoid you as much as possible."

"Too bad you didn't let me in on your decision."

"I couldn't. I was too embarrassed," he said simply.

Donovan—embarrassed? But he looked perfectly serious.

"Why would you be embarrassed?" she asked, needing to hear his answer.

"Because I did the one thing you would never do. I broke my word." He held up a hand when she would have interrupted. "I proposed to you and then I ran away like a scared rabbit. I thought I had good reasons. Those reasons were why I didn't feel I had to face you that day."

"It doesn't matter." But she was curious about his "reasons."

"Yes, Abby, it does, because I'm beginning to think that my reasons for leaving weren't based on fact. If I'd have asked you outright—"

"You would have married me just to keep your word? Thanks a lot."

He shook his head.

"You're not listening, Abby. Ever since fifth grade you've always done exactly what you said. You keep your word, no matter what it costs you."

"Yeah, I'm a paragon. Look what that won me," she said bitterly.

"It's won you the admiration of everyone at Woodwards, not the least of which is my very astute grandmother," he said softly. "It certainly won you my respect."

"So much so that you want to avoid me." That still hurt.

"Because you're the opposite of me. I'm a chicken when it comes to living up to other people's expectations. You of all people know how hard it was for me to keep my word. I always thought up ways to avoid making promises. I fail people. And I feel like a jerk afterward."

Abby had to smile at that. It was such an un-Donovan statement.

"You may not always have kept your word in the past, but you've changed since you've come home. You said God was helping you. And you have gone out of your way to make sure Ariane is safe and comfortable." Abby frowned at him. "So what's the real reason you tried to avoid me, Don?"

He studied her, his blue eyes swirling with clouds. One hand lifted to touch her cheek.

"I didn't want you to be disappointed or change your plans because of me, Abby."

"But why would I do that, unless—" An idea glimmered. "You were afraid I'd think you were home to resurrect the past, weren't you?" She laughed out loud, and if there was a tinge of bitterness in it, well, who cared. "Same old ego, Donovan."

"Not that," he said, shaking his head vehemently. "I wanted to make sure you didn't depend on me. I am not trustworthy, Abby." He sighed. "God willing, I'm trying to change, but it's not easy, you know?"

Abby looked him straight in the eye.

"Let's get something straight, Donovan. I don't expect anything from you. I don't want to change you and I'm not trying to get back at you. The past is over. I'm focused on my future and it lies in New York."

"I know." He didn't look that pleased.

"I'm not holding any grudges about the past. If you want my help, say so. I'll do what I can. I'm a big girl now. I can look after my own feelings." She stretched out her hand. "Deal?"

He didn't smile or joke or do any of the other Donovan things she expected. Instead he leaned forward and brushed his lips against her cheek.

"Deal," he whispered. "Thank you, Abby."

"You're welcome. And now I think we'd better get back to work." She turned her head, caught sight of the house to her right and gulped. "Donovan?"

"Yeah?" He'd shifted the car into gear and was ready to pull away.

"Wait! Look." She pointed. "Heritage House. It's for sale." She turned to see why he wasn't speaking and saw he was totally focused on the house.

His cell phone rang. He answered absently, assuring Katie he was on his way, but his eyes never drifted from the house until Abby giggled.

"That house portrays everything we want to show in our

campaign. Solid. Dependable. Adaptable. Is that the house of your dreams or what?"

"Or what," he agreed. "Write down the number, will you? I'm going to contact the real estate agent to view it." He drove off, but not without a backward glance.

"The stone gives it a wonderful cottagey, yet permanent, feel." Abby couldn't get it out of her head. "And those chimneys. Endurance."

"I like the setting, back from the road on a cul-de-sac and not busy."

"It's not close to your parents," she reminded. "Or your grandmother."

"But not that far from Reese."

"Heritage House." Abby couldn't get the name from her mind.

It sounded like the kind of place where memories had passed down for years and years, where babies came home and children ran laughing and giggling over its expansive yard. A place where family gathered to celebrate its milestones, a place that oozed joy and contentment.

It seemed like a home.

She was still daydreaming when Donovan opened her car door.

"Thanks a lot for coming with me, Abby. I appreciate it."

"Thank you for lunch. My parents are going to welcome you from now on. Especially Mom because she hates cooking."

"I'm not so sure about that." He wore a strangely quizzical look.

Abby had no idea what he meant, but didn't have time to think about it. She had three clients waiting and a ton of messages to return.

Although Abby worked hard to complete each task, thoughts of Heritage House kept returning to her mind. Especially one certain image of her at the doorstep with Donovan.

Now where had that come from?

Chapter Seven

"You're kidding me." Donovan frowned as the realtor explained that Heritage House had been sold a few hours earlier.

"It's a gorgeous home. We've had a lot of people interested and it went fast. Shall I keep an eye out for something else for you?"

Suddenly house hunting lost its joy. But he couldn't give up.

"Sure. E-mail me with anything that's similar to Heritage House."

Donovan hung up the phone only to find a blank planning page staring up at him. Why couldn't he get in the swing of things? Where had all the ideas that had teased his brain for weeks on end gone?

"Hi, honey. You look a bit down." Fiona handed him a cup of coffee. "Anything wrong?"

"No. Just that I found a house, the perfect house, but it's already sold." He set the coffee aside, not really interested in it so soon after lunch.

"Well, as it happens, I might be able to help you out." His mother spread out an array of papers. "This is a list of houses your father and I thought might be suitable. They're all in the range you talked about and with decent neighborhoods."

"Mom, you didn't have to do that." He scanned the sheets, noticed that all of the homes were near his parents' home. None of them struck him as strongly as Heritage House had. "This was really nice of you."

"I particularly chose the first three because of the space in the backyard. Ariane is going to want plenty of room and those three all have pools."

"Oh. Yeah. Great." He hadn't even considered a pool.

"If they don't suit, I can find plenty more for you. But that can't be the only thing that's bugging you." Fiona pushed the hair off his forehead as she had when he was two. "What else has you chewing the ends off pencils?" She held up three to demonstrate.

"It's this campaign Grandmother wants Abby and I to come up with for the jewelry department." He waved a hand at the display board where he'd laid out past publicity efforts Weddings by Woodwards had used. "I can't seem to click on anything that she likes."

"Well, don't use this one." Fiona pulled a clipping off the board. "It was an abysmal failure. And those two weren't much better."

"Thanks," he muttered. "So what *should* I use? Any ideas?"

"Something flashy, hip. Eye-catching, but not weird." She named several ads she'd seen on television. "They snag you right off. That's what we need. Why not use a wedding setting? That's what we're about after all."

"Grandmother didn't like the idea."

"So change it. Spice it up. Bring in a big name."

"That's good." Images began to fly through his head and Donovan scrawled down ideas.

"I thought Abby was helping with that project."

"She is. But she's not a marketer. I am. I have to get the ideas down."

"I don't want to pry, son, but did you ever talk to her about your conversation with her mother on grad night, about Abby going to New York?"

"There was no scholarship, Mom. That part was a lie."

"And the rest?"

"I don't know yet. I'm trying not to ruffle any feathers, but I am going to find out the truth."

"Why don't you just tell her what you were told?"

Donovan shook his head.

"Abby's relationship with her mother is already rocky. I don't want to make it worse for Abby." He grinned. "Besides, Mrs. Franklin was almost friendly the last time I was at her condo. She wants to teach Ariane piano."

Fiona's lips pursed.

"Donovan, I'm trying not to pry, but do you still have feelings for Abby?"

"We've both moved on," he said, using Abby's line. His mother seemed satisfied with that and left his office.

But the truth was Donovan was no longer sure of what he felt. In Europe he'd been able to shove Abby and the perfidy he was sure she'd committed, the disloyalty to their shared dream that her mother had confirmed, out of his thoughts while he buried himself in work. George had helped. So had Ariane.

But Abby had never moved far from his mind and in those odd moments when he let his brain wander, he'd wondered why she was still in Denver when her goal had always been to move to New York.

Now finding answers to the questions he'd entertained in Paris had become more important. But he still hesitated to ask her outright. What if she said it wasn't a mistake, that she really hadn't wanted to marry him?

Five years ago he'd been devastated when Mary Franklin had told him Abby had only agreed to marry him because she didn't want to hurt him, that she'd already made plans to pursue her dreams. She'd shown him Abby's airline ticket and a letter that said she'd won a full scholarship. Donovan had read them and felt sick. He thought they'd shared everything, but Abby hadn't even told him she was applying to that college.

A hard knock on the door broke into his reminiscences.

"Abby. What's up?"

When she didn't answer, Donovan took a second look. Something was brewing in those dark eyes.

"When we were talking—you said you thought you had a good reason for leaving for Europe. That's why you didn't feel you had to explain to me." Her serious eyes held his gaze. "I was wondering—could you tell me what that reason was?"

Donovan caught his breath. Why hadn't he just shut up?

She had a life, a goal, plans. She'd repeated over and over that the past was finished, that she was focused on New York. It was just taking longer, that's all. It didn't mean she felt anything toward him.

"I thought you didn't want to hark back to the past?"

"I don't," she admitted, but the shadows in her eyes remained. "I just thought—" After a short pause Abby shook her head. "Never mind. Tell me about Heritage House. Did you call?"

"Yeah." He grimaced, hiding his relief at not having to explain. "Sold. I guess I keep looking."

"Sold? Oh." She blinked, shook her head. The glint of green-gold in her brown eyes fizzled away. "I never even considered that. What are those?"

"Some listings Fiona found." He waited as she scanned the pages. "Not exactly on par with Heritage House, are they?"

"Not even close." Abby set down the papers and studied him. "Are you going to look at them?"

He shrugged. "I suppose. After all, she's already done a lot of the work and these are at least in my price range."

"I see."

Even though Abby didn't say anything else, he had the distinct sense she wanted to. And judging by the glint in her eyes, it wasn't something he wanted to hear. So he changed the subject.

"What are you working on this afternoon?"

"Ariane gave me an idea for a bracelet. I was trying to put together a prototype, but it's not working."

"I know the feeling." He pointed to his list. "Mom suggested I take the wedding idea from that commercial and try a new slant."

"But I thought—" Abby stopped, pressing her lips together in a determined line.

Donovan could guess what she was going to say so he smiled and inclined his head. "Say it," he invited.

"I thought your grandmother wanted something new, something fresh. Not a remake of an old idea."

"She does." But it had been easier to accept his mother's advice. Just as it seemed easier to look at the homes she'd selected from the Realtor's pages than do the legwork himself.

"Donovan?" Abby's troubled hazel eyes studied him. "I didn't mean to discount your ideas."

"No. It's okay. I was just realizing how simple it always is to let myself take the easy route."

"Huh?" She might pretend not to understand, but Donovan had an idea Abby had already seen what he was only now glimpsing in himself.

"My family has been too ready to run to my rescue since I've come back, probably because they want me to stick around. I guess they've always done it. I've let them, too," he admitted, "from coercing my sisters to feeding us to asking Reese to cover for me, to letting you do most of the brainstorming for the jewelry department. I've avoided responsibility that would have taught me how to become a stronger and more competent individual, instead of allowing me to skate over my problems."

"So now you know. That's a good thing, isn't it?" She smiled.

"Yes, it's good. It's something God has been showing me

little by little, ever since George died. I think it's to help me grow and take control of my world instead of letting things happen and then ducking and running when it gets tough. I've only begun to realize that it applies to everything I do. God expects me to do my best for Weddings by Woodwards, for Winifred and for Ariane."

Donovan crumpled up his brainstorming list and tossed it into the nearby garbage container.

"Good for you." Abby's smile was the best praise he could have asked for. "You know, that reminds me of something Art told me. It was a verse he found in the Bible, but he used a newer translation. Something about being a new and different person with 'a freshness in all you do and think.'"

"You're reciting the Bible now?" Donovan tried to hide his surprise.

"No, but I thought the verse might help you." Abby's face glowed fire-red and she refused to look at him.

He climbed off his stool and stood beside her, resting one hand on her shoulder.

"It does help me. Thank you, Abby. I'm trying to be the person God wants me to be and that verse helps me see he doesn't want me to take the easy way in any part of my life. Freshness is all about tossing out the old and finding a better way."

She studied him for several moments.

"How do you figure out who the person God wants you to be is?" The quietness of her voice and the unsure timbre of her words demanded a serious response.

"You have to keep constantly in touch with him and keep checking everything against his word." He smiled to soften his words. "And sometimes he uses someone, like you, to make me aware of faulty thinking."

"It would be easier if he gave you a list and you could check off the items."

"Easier, maybe. But oh-so-boring and unfresh." He moved

his hand, conscious of the way Abby seemed to freeze whenever he got too close. "What about you? Anything happening with your contest entries?"

"I have lots of ideas, even several projects I want to do." She frowned, twirled a piece of hair with one finger. "But I can't think of anything to tie them together."

"Tell me the projects you're considering. Maybe I can think of something."

"A child's bracelet that includes some kind of hidden identity feature. You know, a special gift but with purpose. An anniversary necklace that lets you keep adding to it as the years pass. A unique watch bracelet for high school graduates. Stuff like that." She frowned at him. "What do you think? Be honest."

"I think you have great ideas. But I have no clue as to how you can tie them together. Sorry." And he was, especially because Abby looked so deflated. Maybe he could cheer her up. "Today is ice-cream day. You up for it?"

"Ice cream? Oh, you mean Ari and her new friend." She grinned. "Scared?"

"Totally," he admitted without rancor. "You have to come and support me."

"But then you'd be outnumbered by females three to one."

"So you can explain the female psyche to me." She was weakening and they both knew it. "Come on, Abby. Please?"

"I'm supposed to be working."

"You worked four hours of overtime last night with that client who wanted the necklace to wear to her party." He grinned. "Katie told me. Woodwards owes you some free time."

"A person can never keep a secret around here," she grumped.

"Besides, we can brainstorm some new ideas while we're there." God wouldn't think he was avoiding responsibility if Abby came along, would he?

Her delightful smile reappeared.

"You know very well we won't get any work done." She chuckled at his shame-faced look. "Okay, I'll come, but be warned that I will be very busy for the rest of the week working off all those calories."

"Like you have to worry." Donovan admired the way her cream sheath hinted at her curves. "We'll leave as soon as Ariane arrives from school."

"I'd better get busy then." She waved a hand and left his office, her heels clicking against the shiny hardwood.

"I thought you told me your plan was to avoid Abby," Reese murmured as he stepped through the doorway. "Now you're going for ice cream together?"

"She's helping me with Ariane and a friend." Avoid Abby—he was beginning to realize how impossible that was.

"Watch yourself this time, Don. You cannot hurt Abby again."

"I know. Anyway, it's not like that. We're just friends."

Reese shot him an odd look but said nothing other than, "Here are some notes from Grandmother."

When the room was empty, Donovan closed the door. He sat down at his worktable, but no new vision filled his brain. Instead he saw Abby, head tossed back, laughing. Something inside him burned.

"Lord, you know I don't want to hurt her, but I can't ignore Abby or pretend we weren't close in the past. That would be wrong. But what's right? How can I keep my distance and yet still be there for her?"

He waited for a soft nudge of assurance that God had heard and would answer soon.

But his mind echoed back two questions. Why was it so important to keep his distance? Was he afraid to get too close because he knew Abby wasn't staying in Denver but moving on to New York? This time he'd be the one left behind.

That thought was so ugly Donovan pulled out his pad and forced his brain to start issuing marketing ideas.

Whatever the answers to those questions, he did not want to probe them right now.

Happiness was contagious; Abby giggled right along with Ariane and her friend Jessica.

She laughed until Donovan handed her a cone that was definitely not filled with butter pecan ice cream.

"Be a new and different person with 'a freshness in all you do,' remember?" He grinned as she timidly accepted the cone. "Try it."

"It's not something weird like Gobi berries and sweet grass, is it?"

"Taste it first, then I'll tell." He handed the girls their cotton candy cones and sat down opposite Abby. "Well?"

Abby obediently took one lick and waited. A delicious tangy sweetness filled her mouth. She tried another taste and found it equally delectable.

"I'm guessing she likes it." Donovan winked at the girls who giggled some more.

"It's wonderful. What's it called?" Abby asked.

"Tropical tease," he said with a triumphant smirk. "Contains orange, coconut, banana and pineapple."

"Very tropical. And very good. But why is it that you have plain old chocolate? Aren't you the guy who's changing his image?"

"I'll have you know this is perfectly proper chocolate pistachio."

"Puh-leeze." Abby gave him a droll look which Ariane and Jessica mimicked. "At least get a scoop of something unusual on top. I can do that for you." She lifted the cone from his hand and moved to the counter where Tiffany obligingly added a large dollop of what she called lemon licorice on top. "Try that," she urged handing the cone back to him.

Donovan accepted his new ice-cream treat with reservation. After some poking in the ribs from Ariane, he finally tasted it. His face contorted, he grabbed his throat and made a gagging sound.

Ariane grinned as if it was all a big joke, but Abby wasn't so certain. Perhaps he was allergic to something. When the gagging didn't stop, she quickly whisked the top scoop of ice cream onto a napkin.

"There. It should be okay now," Abby said.

Donovan's recovery was instantaneous. He accepted the cone, tasted it and grinned. "Delicious."

"Ooh." Abby ignored the girls' smiles. "You scared me."

"Rule number one. Never touch my ice cream." He nodded when Jessica asked if they could eat at a table outside the window they sat beside. "But don't go anywhere else."

Ariane's quick nod of agreement made Abby realize just how much the girl was changing. She didn't hold back in fear with her new friend in tow.

"She's improving, isn't she?"

"By baby steps. It's embarrassing that it took me so long to see how much she needs other people in her life." He looked thoroughly miserable. "I don't know what would have happened if you and Grandmother hadn't pushed me."

"You would have managed just fine on your own." Abby finished her cone, then wiped her hands on a napkin. "How's the national campaign going?"

"It's not. And that's also embarrassing. The only good thing is that with Winifred away, I don't have to answer her questions about it every single day. She's too busy in her own world." His frown emphasized the storm clouds in his eyes. "I don't know why I can't get in the groove, but nothing seems to work."

"Stop pushing," Abby advised. "Your muse will return. You haven't changed that much."

"What about you? How are your contest entries?"

Abby wiggled in her seat, trying to hide her excitement.

"My ring won the first round. I get to go to New York."

"All right!" Donovan grinned as if it was his own personal victory. "I knew that ring was amazing. But why haven't you told anyone? Or have you?" His smile faded, replaced by a frown. "Am I the last to know?"

"I haven't told anyone else," she reassured him, hiding her eyes. "I wanted to enjoy it for a bit." And take a breather from the inevitable question of "What else are you doing?"

"Then I'm delighted you shared it with me first. Congratulations." Donovan leaned across the table and brushed his lips against her cheek. "It's an awesome start, Abby. What else will you do? Have you got your designs solidified?"

Her fingers drifted to the cheek he'd kissed. She stared at him. "Abby?"

Those dratted memories. She refocused.

"I'm doing two of the designs I told you about. I'm still not sure where I'm going with a theme, but I know it will include those two. It's the rest I'm having problems with."

"How so?" His ice cream finished, Donovan leaned his elbows on the table and cupped his chin in his hands, ready to listen.

That part of Donovan hadn't changed one whit. He was still so generous with his time, willing to hear and maybe offer advice if he could. Abby had missed that, missed the opportunity to be totally honest with someone.

Well, *almost* totally honest.

"That fierce scowl tells me something's really bugging you. Want to share?" He waved at the girls, held up a napkin and dabbed his chin to point out that Ariane was wearing her ice cream. "Come on, Abby. Talk."

She was about to unload on him when his cell phone rang.

"Sorry." He clicked it on. After greeting the caller, Donovan fell silent. His face metamorphosed from disbelief, to incredulity, to delight. "Yes, I am. When?" He listened some more, nodded and hung up. "Do you have to go straight back to work, Abby?" he asked, blue eyes shiny, clear and sparkling with excitement.

"Why?"

"Heritage House is back on the market. Apparently the other deal fell through and the agent says the owners want a quick sell because they've already moved. We can go look through it now, if you've got time. Do you?"

To look through the house that had captured her imagination from the moment she'd spotted it behind those charming old maple trees—yes, Abby had time for that.

They collected the girls, cleaned off as much ice cream from their sticky fingers as possible and drove to the house while Donovan explained the trip to the children.

Heritage House was just as enchanting the second time around. Even more so as Abby noticed the long circular driveway guarded by Lombardy poplars standing like stately sentries.

"It will be a lot of work in winter. I might have to buy a snowblower."

Abby couldn't respond. She was too busy admiring a little rose arbor to the left of the house, a birdbath and waterfall to the right, all tucked in among an English country garden that boasted a wealth of flowers. Beyond that, a hedge of heady lilacs in full bloom guarded the rear of the house from view.

"Privacy and beauty. It's gorgeous."

"It's big." Donovan pulled up to the front door, parked and shut off the engine. His face paled. "It's very big."

"It's roomy," Abby agreed as the girls climbed out of the car and raced across the lawn to look at some robins flocking to a feeder in the midst of the flowers. "But not overly big. From here the stone looks in good repair. Low maintenance."

Overall the house had a kind of timeless look, as if it had been there forever, nurturing families through thick and thin.

"Aren't you going to get out?" she asked when it seemed Donovan would never move.

"Yes. Of course." He joined her at the front door as the real estate agent emerged.

"I'm awfully sorry. I have to leave. My child has been injured at school. Would you like to reschedule," she said in a harried voice.

Donovan seemed dumbstruck, so Abby stepped forward.

"We're so sorry to hear that. Why don't you go ahead? Perhaps we can look through ourselves and lock the front door as we leave. Would that be all right? Donovan's so excited to see inside. I'm sure you have his number at Weddings by Woodwards."

"I do. It is a lovely house," the woman said, obviously undecided. Then she nodded once. "Yes. That will be fine. I'll stop by to check on things later. Thank you."

"It's not a problem. I hope everything turns out well."

"So do I." The woman scurried away without a backward look, leaving the front door ajar.

The two girls raced up to stand beside them. Ariane stared at the stone turret, eyes huge. A smile tugged at the corner of her lips. She turned to look at Donovan who was also staring at the house, but not with the same excitement. Ariane tugged his sleeve, pointed to the open door when he finally looked at her.

"Shall we go inside?" Abby prompted. What was wrong with him?

"Uh, yeah. Sure." He walked slowly toward the door, his steps halting, unsure.

Abby couldn't understand his demeanor. The house was fantastic. Ariane seemed to like it. As far as she could tell from the exterior, it didn't need a lot of work. Why wasn't Donovan more excited?

They stepped into a large open foyer that displayed semi-circular stairs to the second floor. Underneath the stairs, two massive closets offered plenty of room to tuck away winter coats and boots. The entry floor was flagstone, guaranteed to withstand plenty of all-weather traffic. On either side lay the living and dining rooms.

"Donovan?" Abby touched his shoulder.

"Yes?" When he turned to face her, she caught her breath. He looked dazed.

Because Donovan offered no direction and because Abby didn't want the girls to catch on to his odd mood, she told them to explore, but warned them not to touch anything. Only looking would be allowed. Ariane grinned, nodded and after lacing her hand in Jessica's, they left to look through the house.

"Donovan, what's wrong?"

"Nothing," he said, but she knew he was lying. "Let's take a look, shall we?" He stepped hesitantly into the living room.

Abby followed, completely baffled.

"The place has a very strong presence, doesn't it? Look at the fireplace. You can imagine stockings hung on that mantel and sparks from a lovely fire tumbling onto that marble hearth." She could have gone on, but Donovan had moved to the dining room.

"It's big," was the only comment he offered.

"Which is a good thing. You could easily serve fifteen to twenty people in here. Wonderful family meals," she prodded, searching for some expression in his eyes. She didn't find it. "I guess the kitchen is next door."

"Yes."

Even though Donovan seemed unmoved by the kitchen, Abby couldn't stem her excitement.

"It's fantastic! Look, another fireplace."

Except this one was at eye level, allowing it to be enjoyed by both cook and those seated in the glass-surrounded eating nook. The cabinets were a rich dark wood. The appliances were restaurant-quality stainless, but they did not detract from the feel of comfort in the big room.

"There's a solarium back here, Donovan. Look at the herbs."

So enthused was Abby that she laced her fingers through his as she had so long ago, and tugged him into the room the kitchen overlooked.

"I'm not a gardener," was all he said. But she knew the

moment his interest level rose—when it landed on the pretty pool in the backyard.

Outside Abby couldn't stem her excitement. The yard was completely enclosed, but that was barely noticeable because it had been laid out so charmingly. A flagstone patio held a table and chairs and an outdoor kitchen. It kept going, leading them down a path to a playhouse tucked to one side, which Ariane and Jessica had already found.

Children's play equipment lay beyond, surrounded by lush green grass. To the left, the pool, sparkling azure blue in the sunlight, begged them to jump in, and if you weren't swayed by it, a hot tub added even more temptation.

"There's a security fence around the pool so you wouldn't have to worry about Ariane accidentally falling in," she murmured, twisting to see Donovan's reaction.

His face paled even more.

"Let's go inside."

"Sure." Abby followed, completely stymied by his reaction.

They found a study and huge family room on the other side of the kitchen. Upstairs, four large bedrooms and three bathrooms were in perfect repair. The master bedroom, set in the turret, overlooked the backyard. Abby found no fault with its appointments. The top floor was a child's fantasy.

"What do you think?" Abby asked, concerned by Donovan's rigid expression.

"I think I need to get out of here." His last two words were overridden by childish laughter as Ariane and Jessica chased each other from room to room. Donovan's gaze rested on the little girl who seldom showed any emotion.

Now Ariane's face glowed with joy, her eyes danced with happiness. She grabbed his arm and pointed out the window to the play set at the back.

"Yes, you can play there for a few minutes. But stay away from the pool."

Ariane nodded, grabbed Jessica's hand and raced away.

"Look at her, Don. She's totally comfortable here. There's no fear in her eyes now. She looks perfectly at home."

"I know." The words emerged so softly Abby barely heard them. He led the way down the stairs and to the sunroom at the rear where they stood and watched the two girls. "Believe me, I know."

"What's wrong? Please tell me."

Donovan remained silent for a long time and when he eventually met her gaze, his eyes were tortured.

"Tell me," she repeated.

"This house." He struggled to find the words, but Abby remained silent, waiting. "I think she likes this house because of its stone structure, the turrets, the fireplaces—they remind her of her apartment building in Europe. I think Ariane feels at home here."

"And that's bad?"

"Yes."

Abby knew something was very wrong, but she couldn't understand what. Donovan had been excited to come here. He'd wanted to see the house. But something had changed the moment they arrived.

"You don't like Heritage House?" she asked, confused by the way he'd seemed charmed yet afraid.

"I like it very much. That's not the problem."

"Then what is? You have to tell me because I'm just not getting it."

"It feels like a forever kind of house."

The half whisper shocked her.

"I'm not a forever kind of guy, Abby. You, more than anyone, know that."

Donovan was afraid of being tied down. It was what had driven him to run to Europe, it was what kept him there and it was what still prevented him from embracing a secure future with Ariane.

The knowledge filled Abby with a clarity that helped her understand what he must be going through.

"I don't think I can do this." He rose, glanced around as if he was pursued.

"You can't run anymore, Donovan." Abby stayed still, knowing he had to face the issue for himself. "Tell me the problem."

He stood immobile.

"Is it this house? Is it too expensive?"

"No. It's expensive, but it's not overpriced and I can afford it. Ariane loves it."

"But you don't?"

"I like it." He relaxed slightly, studied the sunroom and kitchen. "It feels—comfortable."

"So what's the problem?" she asked. A fragment of a previous conversation returned. "Didn't you tell me you were relying on God to see you through your life? Didn't you say he would lead you?"

"Yes." He studied her with a frown. "You're defending God?"

If only it was that simple. But deep inside her heart, Abby had too many questions about God, about his place in a person's life, about how he worked. She'd hoped Donovan could answer her questions, but now wasn't the time.

"I'm neither defending nor accusing. I'm just wondering why now, when you've found a place eminently suitable for you and Ari, you suddenly get the jitters. Don't you trust God anymore? Can't he be depended on to help you take this step?"

Abby held her breath, hoping Donovan would say yes because she desperately needed him to stand by his faith.

Then maybe he could share it with her.

Chapter Eight

Could he trust God?

Abby's innocent question forced Donovan to realize something he hadn't thought about until now.

Trusting God wasn't a one-time thing. Because he'd trusted God last week or last month didn't mean he didn't have to reaffirm that trust today and probably tomorrow, and next week as well. And if he trusted God, truly trusted him to lead and guide his life, this fear that grabbed his gut and squeezed so tightly he could hardly breathe, then that fear was wrong.

"I trust him," he said meeting Abby's curious gaze as his heart swelled with courage. "I trust him with my life."

"How can you?" she asked. "How can you just let go and trust in something, someone you can't see or hear?"

"I hear him every time I open my Bible, Abby. I see him in those lilacs and in the roses. I see him in Ariane. And in you."

"In me?" She frowned as if he was teasing her. "How can you see God in me?"

"I see it in the way you comfort Ariane when she's feeling insecure. I see it in the way you care for your parents and I see it in your designs. Who but God could have given you a mind to create such glorious things?"

She stared at him as if he'd sprouted two heads.

"I mean it, Abby. Who but God could have placed the desire in you to create? You should have followed in your parents' footsteps."

"Don't you start."

"I won't," he promised with a smile. "But you have to admit, you have a whole different way of viewing the world. I think that's God at work."

"Then I wish he'd tell me the rest of his plan because I haven't got much time left to send in my project." She glared at Donovan as if it was his fault.

And maybe it was. Donovan had never talked much about God with her. Until now.

"Have you asked him, Abby?" He saw her skepticism, but pressed on anyway. "I mean it. In the Bible it tells us that we'll find God when we seek him. It also says if we ask him, he'll answer. Maybe you should ask God what your next step should be."

Whatever Abby would have responded was cut off by the return of the real estate agent. "Oh, you're still here. Everything okay?"

"Yes, fine. How is your child?" Donovan asked.

"A mere scrape." She tossed off the question and grinned. "I see your daughter is enjoying the playhouse."

"Yes." He made no attempt to correct her because for all intents and purposes, Ariane *was* his child. And it was up to him, with God's help, to provide a real home for her, a place where she could feel secure no matter what happened. Funny, but wherever he looked in this house, he saw Abby as part of their circle. That wasn't going to happen, he reminded himself. "I'm going to need a few more minutes."

"No problem." The agent nodded. "I want to check the timer on the sprinkler system anyway."

As soon as she'd left, Donovan looked at Abby.

"What do you think of this place?"

"I think it's wonderful, charming and cozy but not cramped, with features that make it feel like a real home that generations have enjoyed. I think Ariane will love it here. And I think her friends will be lining up to be asked over for a visit." She smiled. "In short, I think it's perfect for you."

"Why?"

"Close your eyes."

Donovan obeyed, wondering where she was going with this.

"Now listen. Can you hear the children giggling?" Abby stopped, waited until Jessica's voice rang out. "Can you imagine, in five years when Ariane has a pajama party, the laughter you'll hear? In ten years, when the youth group comes over for snacks and a movie? In fifteen years when she walks down the stairs in her wedding gown?"

The thing was, Donovan could imagine all of it. But in every scene he imagined, Abby stood in the background, smiling, encouraging, applauding and cheering them on.

He was falling in love with her all over again.

"It's a wonderful house, Donovan. It could be everything you want it to be. But you have to be the one to decide."

He opened his eyes and studied the oval of her face, the way her brown hazel eyes glowed with an inner fire. Abby, the girl, had blossomed into a woman who still had a grasp on his heart.

Ari came running in, breathless and grinning, her face happier than he'd seen it for months. Jessica trailed closely behind.

Donovan knelt in front of his goddaughter and took her hands.

"Ariane, would you like us to live in this house? Would you like it to be your home?" He saw the way her gaze swerved to look at Abby, noted the unspoken question. So Ari saw Abby living here, too. Interesting.

Abby touched the girl's cheek, her fingers delicately brushing away the grass bits that clung to her dampened, overheated skin.

"He's asking if this could be your home, Ariane. What do you think?"

Ari's gaze moved back and forth between them. Her forehead wrinkled as she tried to think of a way to express herself. After a moment she grasped both his and Abby's hands and nodded at Jessica to follow as she led them into the kitchen. Then she and Jessica sat on the breakfast bar stools and giggled.

"You'd like to have your breakfast here, is that right?" Abby interpreted, on the same wavelength as the girls.

Ari nodded and grinned, then drew them into the family room. She indicated everyone should sit on the floor in front of the fireplace and mimicked holding a book from which she read.

"Bedtime stories," Donovan guessed, feeling triumphant when she nodded.

The game proceeded through the house, a little pantomime in each room to show how his little girl thought the house should be used. On the top floor, she paused. When Jessica prodded her to show what she thought this room should be, Ari frowned then laid on the floor in one corner.

"Your bed goes there," Abby said.

They guessed the rest of the things she wanted in the room until Ariane stood by a wall near her bed. She drew a square there.

Although he offered several suggestions, Donovan couldn't guess what she wanted.

"Ari, honey, can't you just tell us?" he said at last, frustrated by her growing tenseness.

She shook her head. Big tears welled. Even Jessica couldn't stem her sobs. Finally Abby drew her into her arms and let her weep.

"Sweetie, we've had such a lovely time. Don't let this be the memory we have of today. I don't want to remember you crying in here," Abby said.

Ari jerked away, nodded again and again.

"A memory?" Jessica wrinkled her nose. "Is that it?"

Triumphant, Ari drew a square on the wall.

"It's a picture. You want to put your dad's picture there." Relief filled Donovan. He walked over to the wall, studied it. "I think we'd need a bigger frame. This wall is huge."

Ariane smiled, tranquility restored.

"So you think we should buy this house?" he asked her in all seriousness. Ari nodded, face shining. "Will you be happy here?"

She nodded again, raced over to him and threw her arms around his neck. It was the first time she'd initiated such an intense response and Donovan was overwhelmed by it. His heart thumped a hundred miles an hour as he held her precious body near.

"You'll bring your friends here and help me make popcorn and decorate a Christmas tree with me?"

Ariane leaned back, her eyes huge as she considered the possibilities. Then she grinned and gave an almost-laugh of excitement.

"I think that's a yes," Abby murmured.

Donovan caught the sheen of tears on her cheeks, but she was smiling at him.

"So, have you and your wife decided on the house?" The real estate agent stood in the doorway, her smile slightly forced.

Donovan didn't correct her. He simply nodded.

"We'll take it."

"Wonderful." She led them down the stairs, explaining benefits he hadn't even considered.

In the foyer, Donovan looked at Abby.

"Would you be able to take Jessica home and watch Ari until I get back? I want to get the details nailed down right away."

"Sure." Her agreement was automatic, although Donovan knew she hadn't expected to give up even more of her day for him. But she accepted his car keys without comment.

"I'll catch a ride back with her," he said, nodding toward the real estate agent. "Or I'll get a cab. Whatever. Thank you very much, Abby. I appreciate *all* your insight."

"I'm glad I could be here. I think you're going to make this into a wonderful home. Ariane's so excited that I don't think she'll be able to help talking soon."

"We hope." He hesitated a moment, unsure if this was the right time. But when better? "Abby?"

She looked up. "Yes?"

"I trust Him. You can, too."

God had given him the responsibility to be a parent to Ariane. A great responsibility, but also a great blessing. He and Ari had made their first breakthrough. And that helped Donovan realize he wanted Abby to share his faith.

But friendship was no longer enough.

Chapter Nine

The girls' chatter in the backseats offered Abby a chance to think as she drove back to Woodwards.

And she had a lot to think about—especially because that name Heritage House would not leave her brain. She kept getting pictures in her mind. A couple in their first home, a new baby, a birthday celebration, a graduation gathering, an anniversary, a reunion.

The images piled on top of one another and suddenly Abby knew the gist of her theme for the contest.

Heritage.

They had almost arrived at Weddings by Woodwards when her cell phone rang. Abby pulled over to the curb and answered it.

"Hi, Mom."

"Hello, dear. Do you know how I can contact Donovan?"

"Well, he's looking at a house right now. Why?"

"He promised to bring Ariane over for her first lesson today and she's fifteen minutes late. Your father has a meeting he wants to attend and because I'll have to get started on dinner soon, I don't know what…"

"As it happens, Ariane's with me. I could bring her over if you're sure that's what Don wants."

"Those were the arrangements we made last night. He never informed me that anything had changed."

"Okay, let me call him and then I'll call you right back." She rang Don, heard the chagrin when she mentioned her mother.

"Oh, boy. She's going to be really ticked with me now."

"No, it's okay. I'll take Ariane over and make supper while she's teaching. That way they should be okay for time for whatever meeting Dad wants to go to." She chuckled. "I guess I'm taking back that overtime I worked last night."

"I owe you big time, Abby. Shall I meet you at your parents' condo?"

"Sure." She rang off, then told her mother the plan.

"Are you sure you can manage?"

"I'll be fine. Jessica's going to stay for supper." She drove to her parents' house with dreams for her contest entries spinning through her head.

Ariane smiled when she greeted both Mark and Mary. She nodded eagerly when asked if she wanted to have her first lesson. Abby's father quickly involved Jessica in his beading kit, leaving Abby free to work on the evening meal. Knowing her mother's propensity for lighter evening fare, she put together a soup from some leftover meat and vegetables in the fridge and made some biscuits and a salad.

As she worked, Abby heard her mother pointing out the notes on the keyboard and asking Ariane to repeat them. Abby set down her knife, ready to rescue the speechless girl from her mother's tyranny, but on entering the living room, it was obvious the two had made a compromise. Her mother smiled proudly as Ari poked through the C scale.

"Very good, dear," she praised. "You have a natural talent."

Abby swallowed hard. Why hadn't she ever heard those words? Why couldn't her mother have encouraged her own daughter once? Why did her mother find it so much easier to lavish attention and praise on a stranger?

Donovan's words about her God-given talent to be a designer echoed in her mind. Wouldn't it have been easier if God had created the kind of daughter her parents could be proud of?

Moot point now. All she could hope was that winning the first stage of the contest would lead to a win in the finals and a move to New York. Surely that would prove to her mother that she hadn't wasted herself on her chosen career.

Outside Donovan was paying a cab driver. Abby went to open the door.

"Listen," she whispered as she led him to the doorway of the living room. "Ariane's quite talented."

Ari played the little chorus Mary taught her, delighted by the sound of it. She tried it again and again, glowing at the praise heaped on her.

After the third time, Abby led Donovan into the kitchen.

"Dinner's almost ready. You'll stay, won't you?"

"I shouldn't. In fact I should never have allowed Ari to have lessons here."

"Why?" She frowned and whirled to face him. "She's doing so well."

"Perhaps. But it's not fair to you." Donovan's blue eyes darkened. "I can see how much it hurts to hear your mother praise Ari when all she did was natter at you."

"That is not true, Donovan Woodward!" Mary stood in the doorway, cheeks burning hot. "I did my very best to teach Abigail to play that piano. But she would not apply herself. Claimed she wasn't interested. I tried to force her to learn, but that just made things worse. So I let her quit. Because that was what she wanted."

"You couldn't have found her another teacher, one who might have encouraged her instead of haranguing her?"

"She didn't want to learn." Mary was furious and Donovan didn't look like he'd back down either.

"You harassed and browbeat your own daughter because she wouldn't be what you wanted," he accused. "She could have enjoyed music, but you ruined it for her."

Abby couldn't believe it. Donovan was standing up for her—to her mother?

"How dare you!"

"Stop it, both of you. You're scaring the girls." Abby didn't want to do it, but it seemed the only way to put an end to this argument. "Both of you go into the front room and sit down. Go. Now."

Like recalcitrant children they went, but they sat as far apart as possible. Mark simply glanced from one to the other, his face troubled.

Abby sat down at the piano. She closed her eyes, concentrated for a few moments then lifted her hands to the keys and began playing her favorite nocturne by Chopin. So lost did she become in the music that she forgot where she was until the oven buzzer rang. The song ended abruptly.

"Darling, that was fantastic!" Her mother rose and clapped. "I've never heard it played with more heart. That arpeggio was to die for."

"Thanks, Mom." Abby refused to revel in the praise. Instead she hurried to rescue her baking. "Can we eat now? Dad's going to have to leave soon."

"Yes, of course we'll eat. I assume he's joining us?" Mary glanced at Donovan, reserve and censure still lurking in the back of her eyes.

"I—" He sought out Abby's gaze.

"Yes, Donovan and Ariane and Jessica are eating with us. Let's all sit down. Dad?"

Her father walked into the dining room slowly and stopped right in front of her.

"I have never heard anything so lovely," he said quietly. "I am very proud of you, Abby."

"Thanks, Daddy." The words brought tears she tried to hide by hugging him before she pulled out his chair. "I made soup."

"I like soup." He grinned at her.

Everyone laughed.

The meal was a great success, but quickly ended.

"Don't worry about those dishes, dear. The dishwasher makes quick work of them." Mary handed Ari a little booklet with notes about what to practice and teased Jessica about her beadwork. Donovan she ignored.

As the others walked through the door, she grasped Abby's arm to hold her back.

"I was so moved by your playing, dear. I hope you'll play for us again. Maybe we could manage a duet."

"Don't push it, Mom," Abby teased.

"I won't. I promise." Her voice dropped. "I'm so glad you share my love for music, Abby. It's one of the things I always hoped we'd enjoy together."

One of them?

"I'm glad, too, Mom."

"Did you tell them your news?" Donovan demanded when they emerged outside.

"No. I forgot!" Abby grinned. "I won the first stage of the contest in New York, Mom. With the ring—I showed you a picture, remember?"

"That's very nice, dear. Congratulations."

"It's more than *nice*," Donovan sputtered, indignation showing again. "It's amazing. Your daughter took first place over—how many other entries, Abby?"

"Over four hundred, I think."

"You see? She's a genius at jewelry design." Donovan sounded proud.

"I have no doubt." Mary helped Mark put on the jacket she carried. "We'd better get going now. Thanks so much for the meal, dear. Will we see you Friday as well?"

"Of course."

"Wonderful. And Jessica and Ariane, you come again, too." Somehow they were out on the walk before Abby even noticed.

Her mother hurried her father away and she was left standing awkwardly beside Donovan. She handed him his keys and he clicked open the car locks for the girls to get inside. But he remained where he was, mouth pinched tight, eyes blazing blue.

"That woman!"

Abby chuckled.

"You two always were like oil and water," Abby said. "Come on. I need to get to the office and find out what's happened while I've been away."

"Couldn't she manage to squeak out one nice word about your win?" He shook his head. "Where did you learn to play, anyway?"

"I took lessons for several years. It wasn't easy at first, but eventually I relaxed and found it very enjoyable." She shrugged. "No big deal."

"Yes, it was. It took a lot of courage to get over that hurdle. Good for you."

"Thanks." She was embarrassed by his praise of something she'd kept secret for so long. "I had Jessica call her mom and tell her what had happened, but she has to be home in fifteen minutes. We'd better get moving."

"Yeah." He helped her into the car and drove to the little girl's home without further comment. But Abby knew something was going on under that shaggy, yet elegant, haircut.

Abby managed to hold her questions until they were headed for Woodwards.

"Did you get the house?"

"That rampant curiosity is going to get you into trouble one day," he warned.

She reached out and pinched his arm. "Tell me."

"All things being equal, I should be able to take possession of Heritage House in two weeks."

"Hey, that's great!"

"Yeah." But something told her he wasn't quite as excited as she'd hoped.

"Yeah? What's that mean, Don?" She checked on Ariane and saw that she'd fallen asleep. "Have you changed your mind about moving?"

"No. But it's a bit overwhelming." He glanced over one shoulder, shrugged. "I only hope it's going to make a difference to Ari. This silent thing is really eating into her ability to communicate with other kids now. And teachers. And me."

"I think you might be surprised at the difference the house will make to Ariane. She'll have a place that you two will build together, something that's all her own but that she shares with you." Abby smiled, imagining it. "Working on her room is bound to bring the two of you closer."

"Her room?" His head jerked around, eyes gaping. "What is there to do with her room? We get a bed, a dresser, maybe a desk—don't we?" he said when Abby frowned.

"This is your chance to make this place a home. You have to put some thought into it." She couldn't believe he thought he was past the hardest part of building a home. "You can't pick up any old furniture and plop it in Ariane's bedroom. It's got to be something Ariane really likes and will want to sleep in for years."

"I don't know anything about that stuff."

"Donovan, your entire family is involved in fashion," she chuckled. "I'm sure they'd gladly pitch in and decorate the place for you."

"For me. Those are the operative words. No." He clamped his hands around the steering wheel. "You're right. This has got to be my gig, something I don't go running to them for."

"You could always hire an interior designer."

He made a face.

"And end up decorated? It would be like having Mom take over. Italian sofas, white everything. Totally un-man-friendly and even worse for Ari. Nope, I'm not going that route." He gave her a sideways look. "I'd appreciate your help, though."

"Me?" she squeaked.

"Why not? Your dad said you helped with their place."

"Don, that was a few rooms where we picked out the most comfortable stuff and had it moved in. It wasn't furnishing a whole house. Besides," she said, forcing the words out. "Aren't you supposed to be avoiding me?"

He grimaced.

"I should never have let that out. It's going to haunt me for a long time, I can tell."

"Well, it is what you said."

"And I meant it. Because I thought I would be hurting you. But couldn't we be friends now, or is that asking too much?" He paused, frowning at her. "Abby?"

"I do consider you a friend," she agreed. Obviously whatever love Donovan once had for her was completely dead. "But that isn't the problem."

"Then what is?"

"I've got to get my designs done for the contest. I need every spare minute right now. And you have to have a marketing plan ready for Winifred, don't you?" She waited for his nod. "Do you really have time to decorate a house by yourself right now?"

"I'm going to have to make time," he said, a stubborn tilt to his chin. "This is for Ari, to give her a home with me. Heritage House is the start of our future and I want to make sure it's what we need. I thought you'd be happy for us."

"I am. I really am, Don. I think this is exactly what you should be doing and I'm very proud of you for putting her first."

"Proud?" He blinked. "I don't think you've ever said that about me before."

"Well, I am saying it now. I've never been more proud of you for getting past your fears and doing the right thing."

"I'm not sure I am past them yet," he mumbled as he pulled in beside her car at Woodwards. "Imagining how I'm going to keep that place running by myself and keep Ari happy is sending shivers down my back."

"You'll do it by tackling it one step at a time. And I'll be there—if you really need me." She gave in, knowing very well from the start that that's what she'd intended to do. Somehow, when it came to Donovan she couldn't seem to deny anything he asked of her.

"Until you leave for New York," he said quietly.

"Yes. I'll help you until then." Funny how that thought didn't bring as much joy as it once had.

"Thank you, Abby." He drew her into his arms, hugging her tightly. "I know I'm imposing, but I really don't think I can get through this without you. The family will want to take over and knowing you're in my corner, backing my decisions, will make it easier for me to refuse their help and stand on my own two feet. For once."

"You really have changed." Because it felt too good to relax in his arms, Abby eased away and leaned back to inspect his handsome face. "Either this thing with God that you've got going on is real or you're a much better actor than you used to be."

"My relationship with God is real," he insisted, eyes bright with purpose, "and I've stopped trying to play parts. The prodigal son has finally grown up, Abby, and I intend to face my responsibilities, with God's help."

"Good for you," was the only thing Abby could think of to say. She stepped out of the car and bent to say goodnight. "Tell Ariane I said sweet dreams."

"You, too. And thanks again. I don't know how I would have managed without you." He reached over and brushed his knuckles against her cheek. "I can't imagine how I'll ever repay you, Abby. Without you, I don't think I'd have had the courage to face any of this."

"I'm beginning to realize you would have done just fine, Donovan." She eased back so his hand would drop away. "Goodnight."

Abby walked to her car, unlocked it and climbed inside because she knew he wouldn't leave until he was certain she was safe. But once Donovan pulled out of the parking lot, Abby got out and unlocked the door to Woodwards.

Time was going to get increasingly precious. To have her contest entries ready she'd have to snatch every spare moment.

But as she sat in front of her workbench with her tools and equipment spread around, it dawned on Abby that she would be helping Donovan create a home, something she'd imagined them doing together five years ago.

Only this home wouldn't be hers.

She wasn't going to be his bride, or his wife, or Ariane's stepmother. She wasn't even going to be involved in their lives very much once the house was finished. In fact, if everything went as she hoped, she might not even be here to see him celebrate his first Christmas at Heritage House.

Why did it hurt so much that Donovan needed her now, when he hadn't for five long years?

And how would she ever convince herself she was okay with that?

"Abby?"

The sound of her mother's voice in Weddings by Woodwards, at ten the next morning, took Abby so much by surprise that she almost dropped the bracelet she was working on.

"Mom?" She pulled open her door. Mary stood outside it, twisting the handles of her bag between her fingers. "Is Dad with you? Come in."

"Actually, your father is at his program at the seniors' center this morning. He goes every week."

"Of course. I'd forgotten." The look on her mother's face told her she shouldn't have. "Will you sit down? Can I get you some coffee?"

Abby dealt with those matters while furiously scrabbling through her brain to uncover the reason for this unprecedented visit.

"Is that one of the projects for your contest?"

"Yes, it is." She'd been going to explain the concept, but one glance at her mother's face told her that she was preoccupied with something else. "Is something wrong?"

"No. Well, yes." Mary puffed out a sigh and sipped her coffee. "I need your help, Abby."

"Of course," she answered automatically as her spirit dipped. Donovan was accepting his responsibilities, but she wanted to drop some of hers. Life was getting too full. Then again, nobody had given her a choice. "What is it, Mom?"

"There's a church your father and I have been attending sporadically. I suppose you think that's foolish," she muttered, her cheeks dotted red. "But it seems to help Mark and we both enjoy the fellowship."

"Why would I think that's foolish? I've been trying to encourage you to get out more." Abby couldn't imagine what her two antireligion parents would want at a church, but she wasn't going to say it and initiate another argument.

"Well, we have been getting out. And we like this church. In fact," her mother held her gaze with a steely glare. "I've begun attending a Bible study there."

"Good for you." Now Abby knew where the grace and the Bible reading came from. "So what's the problem?"

"The current study is finished. The next one is scheduled for Friday evenings." Her mother sat straight and stiff in the chair. "I would like to attend."

It took a minute for the words to sink in.

"You'd like me to come and sit with Dad, is that it?"

"If you could." Mary's face lit up and her eyes began to glow. "This minister—he's an amazing teacher, Abby. He explains things so clearly. I've never heard anything like what he talks about."

"Where does this study occur?" Abby asked.

"It's at the same church the Woodwards go to. When we moved into the condo, Winifred Woodward stopped by with a basket of goodies and an invitation to their church. One Sunday we decided to go and we loved it."

Abby had been there to hear Art sing but she hadn't seen her parents.

"I see." What else had Winifred been doing without anyone knowing? "Well, if you want to go and it means this much, I'm sure I can rearrange my schedule. Or maybe I can bring Dad here. I have a whole kit of beads he can work with."

"I'm not sure that's a good thing for Mark to be doing." Disparagement oozed through Mary's soft yet brittle tone.

"Why not? He enjoys it. It keeps his fingers dexterous and he gets to make something pretty. Where's the harm in that, Mother?" Surprised by the spurt of fury rising inside her, Abby told herself to calm down.

"It just seems so—beneath him."

The words stung. As if her work was somehow not good enough to meet the Franklin family standard.

"Beneath him?" she repeated icily.

"Your father was a scientist, Abby. One of the best. To be reduced to—"

Abby lost her cool.

"Reduced to what, Mother? To finding pleasure in something small and innocent? To letting go of the pretense that he can actually crack all the mysteries of the universe and allow himself to enjoy something petty, and dare I say fun? Is that what's bothering you, Mother? Or is it that *you* feel reduced?"

"This work of yours, Abby, it's not—"

"Not your choice for me. I get that, Mother. I know you hate that I'm a simple jewelry designer, that I've never craved to be a scientist who follows in your footsteps. I understand you are disappointed. But isn't it time you accept that I have the right to choose my own future?"

"I'm only saying—"

Abby drew in a deep breath, wishing she'd never begun this discussion, but also aware that it was time to get her feelings out in the open.

"This is who I am, Mom. This is what I do."

"And she's very good at it." Winifred pushed open the door and entered, her smile gentle, as if she'd overheard nothing. "Mary, how nice to see you. How are you and Mark?"

"We're well. I hope you don't mind that I stopped by."

"Of course not. Abby's so willing to put in overtime for us, I could hardly begrudge her a coffee with her mother. I see you're wearing one of my scarves. What struck you most about it?"

"Oh, the color, of course. And the feel of it. Silk is so wonderful against the skin," Mary replied.

"It is, isn't it? That's what so many of our clients say about Abby's work, too. That it just seems to fit them." Winifred picked up the bracelet Abby had been working on and laid it against her wrist. "Take this, for instance. You'd never imagine that it has a little homing device embedded in it, would you? It's so light, yet strongly made so a child won't easily break it. I have no doubt that someday it will save a child's life. All thanks to Abby's creativity."

"Yes, but—" Mary didn't get the next word out.

"It's a wonderful thing to be able to create. I know because I've been doing it for years. It's one of many gifts God gives to his children." Winifred winked. "I suspect you've had the same experience in your work, haven't you, Mary? You suddenly get an idea and nothing anyone can say will stop you from pursuing it?"

Winifred's expectant look was almost embarrassing. Abby cleared her throat.

"We're disturbing you, aren't we, dear? I know you're plowing ahead, preparing for the contest along with all your other work." Winifred patted her shoulder. "Allow me to congratulate you on your entry. First place! That's remarkable. I couldn't be more proud and I want you to take all the time you need to get the rest prepared. You can't possibly drop out now. Not when we're all cheering for you."

With a cheery goodbye and a wave to Mary, Winifred disappeared as quickly as she'd arrived. Abby couldn't think what to say, but her mother could.

"I didn't realize your work would have such a large impact." Her mother's eyes narrowed. "Will you still need that loan we talked about?"

Talked about? They'd promised her.

"Yes, Mom. I will. I did get some help from someone else, but it doesn't cover all the expenses I'll have to finish my contest designs."

"I'll talk to your father."

As if Dad made any of the financial or other decisions. They both knew Mary was completely in charge. Abby said nothing.

"I have to go now." Mary rose, set her cup on the edge of Abby's desk. "So will Friday night work for you?"

Abby almost sighed. Her work could go on hold, but her mother's needs always came first. Was this really what God meant about children obeying their parents?

"I'll make it work. No problem," she added with a touch of irony.

"Thank you, Abby." One thank-you pat to the shoulder and Mary hurried away, her life organized.

If only Abby could manage her own life so easily.

Abby picked up her forceps, but for the first time in her life, jewelry didn't call to her. She couldn't lose herself in her work or blank out her problems by staring into a gem.

Her mother talked to God. Her father wanted to do something at church. The Woodwards all seemed to have a heavenly connection.

Why had God chosen to shut her out?

Chapter Ten

When the questions grew too hard to ignore, Abby always took a break.

This time she left her office, poured herself a cup of coffee in the staff room and carried it out to the tiny patio Woodwards provided for its staff to enjoy a break.

But there was no distraction here. The others had apparently finished their break or found something else to do. No one sat among the lush plants waiting to chatter about nonsensical things. No one listened to the drift of water over pebbles.

Abby tried to close her eyes and relax, to regain the harmony she'd found working on her project, but it was not there. Instead an inner fury tore at her peace.

Although she'd hoped her win with the ring would impress her mother and finally prove her worth, Abby now doubted Mary would ever see value in her work, no matter what she did.

"What's wrong with me?"

There was no answer in the quiet place. Nor had she expected one. Even though she'd been reading her Bible the past few weeks, she'd found no answers to satisfy her many questions. Certainly she'd found no connection to God.

A small toy of Ariane's lay nearby. Abby picked it up, seeing an image of the little girl nestled between Mark and Mary, all three smiling. Guilt wiggled its head at the envy Abby felt for that child's inclusion in her parents' world. It was tempered by a wealth of understanding for the isolation Ari endured because she wouldn't speak. Abby knew all about isolation.

She dropped the toy. Inside her soul, pain and anguish built up to an unbearable level until finally she glanced heavenward.

"Am I unlovable?" she whispered.

A pewter sign hung above a rose arbor.

Those who believe in him will never be disappointed.

"I'm disappointed," Abby murmured so softly even the birds had to lean in to hear. "I'm disappointed I never manage to please her, that I'm never enough. I'm disappointed that even you don't seem bothered enough to hear my prayers. I'm disillusioned with religion—"

"Abby?" Donovan lounged in the doorway. He scrutinized her face for only a second before he knelt before her. "What's wrong?"

She should have pretended. But she couldn't.

"Me." Abby stared into his vivid blue eyes and wondered how she could possibly explain. "Me. I'm what's wrong, Donovan. Why don't I get it?"

His fingers tightened around hers, his face puzzled.

"Get what?" One hand lifted to push her hair back off her face. "What aren't you getting, Abby? You took first place in that contest."

She nodded.

"That was nice, but it was only the beginning of my dreams. In fact, that happens over and over. I never quite get where I'm trying to go." She paused a moment, bit her bottom lip. "Five years of struggling. You've been halfway around the world but I'm still here in Denver. Do you think it's because God hates me, because I'm doing, or have done something wrong?"

"No!" He shook his head as if to add vehemence to his rebuttal. "God does not hate you, Abby. Never."

"Then why is it I'm always dissatisfied? Why am I always on the outside when it comes to my mother? Why can't I get her on my side or get my ideas off the ground?"

"I think you've got a whole bunch of things going on in that question. Let's start at the top."

She could feel him studying her, although Abby did not return his look. She didn't want to see pity in his gaze.

"The relationship problem—that's really your mother's problem, isn't it?"

She frowned.

"Because you aren't who she wants you to be. So how can you change that? Become a physicist?"

"I think we both know that's out," Abby said in a droll tone as she peeked through her lashes. Don was smiling.

"Okay. So you've got this nutty relationship with her that you can't make better because you don't want to be who Mary wants. Now, what are your options?"

"That's just it. I don't have any!" Abby dragged her hands from his, rose and walked over to the fountain.

"You always have options, Abby."

"Like what?" Fed up with everything, she whirled to face him. "Name some."

"Maintain the status quo?" He rose, leaned against one of the pergola supports. "I don't think you really want that."

"To continue to be the doormat? No, thanks, I'll pass." She sighed, dashed some water on the stones. "Look, forget this. I have too much to do to sit around out here, hashing this over."

"Sometimes it is necessary to hash over stuff to sort out our minds." Donovan studied the little plaque with a speculative glance. "Why would you think God hates you?"

Abby laughed bitterly.

"Look around, Donovan. You have what you came home for.

Ariane isn't speaking yet, but she will soon. You'll soon have your house, you're doing the job you wanted, and you're putting together your campaign."

"Not quite." He rolled his eyes. "But keep going."

"Look at your parents, your family then. Maybe I shouldn't say this," she muttered, cheeks burning under his scrutiny, "but you all seem to move merrily through life with God's blessing on you. I'm not saying your grandmother hasn't worked hard for what she has, but it's like she walks under the umbrella of God's grace. You know?"

A boisterous chuckle shook his whole body, but he nodded.

"The charmed life. Grandmother seems like that to me sometimes, too," he agreed, sobering. "But nobody's life is as simple as it seems, Abby. Everyone has rough spots."

"I know that. But still. It's as if your family prays and zap! God answers. I've spent ages praying and never received an answer to my prayers. Maybe what I'm really asking," she paused, hesitant to say the words.

"Yeah?"

"How do I fix my faith?"

At first she thought he'd laugh at her, but when Donovan lifted his head, Abby could see he was seriously considering the question.

"You really mean how do you get God to do what you want." Challenge underlay his quietly spoken words.

"Yes. I guess so." Now it was said, Abby wasn't backing down. She sat in one of the cane chairs and sipped her cooled coffee, waiting for his response. Surely Donovan, with all his years of attending church should have some answers. "Your family is the one who's heavy into this faith stuff. So tell me."

Donovan sat, too, slowly, thoughtfully.

"Abby, I don't think you fix your faith. I think your faith is supposed to fix you."

"Okay. How?" She crossed her arms over her chest and

waited. She was a fairly bright person, she could reason, understand. So she could get this if she tried. "Well?"

"I'm no minister," he began.

"I don't want to talk to one. I just want to understand how God works."

"Like I can explain God in ten minutes? You're always in a hurry, Abby." Donovan let out a long-suffering sigh. "Okay, I'll explain it as I understand it." He leaned forward. "We all want something. But God wants something, too. Sometimes it's the same as we want, sometimes not."

"He doesn't want me to design jewelry?" Abby frowned. "But I thought you said that's what I was created for? Or maybe it was Winifred. Anyway, why would I be—?"

"Wait a minute, will you?" Exasperation touched Donovan's bright eyes. "I can't say what God wants you to do, Abby. Neither can Grandmother or you. That's for him to tell you."

"How, if he never answers me?"

Donovan smiled as if he knew a great secret.

"God always answers, Abigail. Always. Sometimes we have to wait until the voices in our own minds are all shut down so we can truly listen. But if we wait long enough, he promises he will always tell us what we need to hear."

"That's it?" Incredulity didn't begin to describe her frustration level. "You're telling me to wait and eventually, somehow, somewhere, I'll figure out what God's trying to tell me?" She glared at him. "You can't be serious!"

"I'm very serious. You have to get your soul to a place where it can hear God, a place where you're not in control, yelling your demands. God isn't your servant and he will only speak when he's ready, when he decides you're ready to listen to him."

"But—"

"It isn't easy and it isn't fast, but that's the only way I know to find God's will. Ask and then shut up and listen."

"I've got a contest to enter. A life to live. Decisions to make," she snapped. "I can't sit and wait for enlightenment to dawn."

"Then you won't hear him speak." Donovan glanced at his ringing cell phone and shrugged. "Gotta go."

Abby closed her lips, blinked when he stopped mid-stride and asked the person to wait.

"One more thing." Donovan held his palm over his phone, his expression serious. "When you ask God a question, make sure you want to hear the answer, Abby. Sometimes it is not what you expect."

"Thanks."

He smiled.

"Don't look so forlorn. God is knowable. The Bible says faith comes by hearing and hearing comes through God's word. If you want to know him, read his letter to you, the Bible. Later."

Then he was gone and once more she was alone.

Abby stared at the sign above the rose arbor.

"Okay," she muttered, forcing herself to utter the words. "I'll listen. I need some answers. Can you do that? Please?"

She didn't expect anything immediate, so she returned to the staff room, washed and replaced her cup and went back to her office. That's when she noticed she'd sketched "Bible Study" onto her calendar.

Maybe it was time to find her own Bible study where she could learn how to listen to God. The newspaper offered suggestions and Abby soon had her decision made. It would cost another evening of her time, but surely figuring out what and how she believed was worth the sacrifice?

Abby picked up her tools and began working, new hope springing inside.

"Abby?"

Donovan switched on the lights of her office, unable to believe she wasn't here. So much for planned confrontations.

On top of Abby's desk lay a length of silver chain, shaped into one word.

Heritage?

What did his house have to do with her work?

"Donovan?"

He whirled around in surprise. Abby stood behind him, forehead pleated in a frown.

"Were you looking for me?"

"Yes," he blurted only then realizing how what he'd been about to say would sound to her.

I was worried about our conversation this afternoon so I planned some one-on-one time with you. Abby would not appreciate that.

"Well, now you've found me." She removed her jacket and hung it up before setting out her tools. "Is it enough to see me or did you want to talk also?" she teased.

"How's the contest coming?" It was the first thing he'd thought of.

"Fine. You know I'm beginning to wish I'd never told anyone. Everyone keeps asking me that. So I'll turn the tables. How's the marketing campaign coming along?"

"It's not." He flopped down on the guest chair and reached out to trace the chain. "What's this?"

Abby blushed. He couldn't believe it. She seldom lost her composure and yet this little bit of chain turned her golden tanned skin a dark embarrassed red.

"Something to do with the house?" he probed, curiosity aroused.

"Not exactly." She turned her back to him, pretended to dig for some tools. "I'm going to use it as my concept theme. You can take credit for it if you want."

"Me?"

"Because of your house. Heritage House. That name played

on my mind until I decided it fit my ideas perfectly." She laid out some display boards. "What do you think?"

There were five boards in all. Each one displayed a piece of jewelry she'd created. Donovan couldn't stop staring.

"It's fantastic!"

"Thanks. I think it will work." Abby laid out several pieces. "These two are finished. The rest are prototypes. My slogan will be something like, *Our heritage, your future.*"

He stared at her.

"Ever think about changing jobs?"

"Recently, a lot." A puzzled look washed over her face. "What do you mean? Don't you think it will work?"

"It will work. It's a PR dream, a marketing coup. It embodies everything about Woodwards. You should have my job."

"No, thanks." She wrinkled her nose. "My own is enough."

Ideas mushroomed so fast Donovan had to grab a pad and start writing.

"It will work with nostalgia but bumped up by modernity— Grandmother's deepest wish. It will grab everyone's attention. There are a thousand ways to go with this."

Abby moved to look over his shoulder, suggested a couple of changes to his notes and tweaked others. Then she grew silent. Suddenly Donovan realized what he'd done.

"I apologize, Abby. Here I am usurping your idea and I truly didn't mean to do that. It's yours, for your contest, and I have no business trying to use it."

"These are for the jewelry department. How about Generations? It encompasses everything we want and all of those ideas you've written down will work with it." She grinned. "See, I told you that house would be important."

"Yes, you did. And once again, you are right, Abigail Franklin. Absolutely right."

She pretended to ignore him, but he could see the pleasure in her face as she worked on the watch bracelet.

"Why don't you make the strap look like a path—you know, steps taken to the end of a journey?" Seeing her frown, Donovan wished he'd kept silent. What did he know about making jewelry?

But Abby quickly reformed the bracelet, adding little touches to it until it quickly became something beyond what he'd imagined.

"Is that what you mean?"

"It's perfect. You could do a diamond for each hour on the watch faces."

"Been done." She thought a moment then placed an arrangement of tiny colored paste bits like stepping stones. "Better?"

"Yes."

The bracelet translated in his mind to a graduation gown, homecoming and prom queen tiaras. He sketched and drew as Abby worked nearby, neither of them saying anything to the other. There was no need to talk.

He'd been worried she was depressed, that she'd given up on the contest. He'd come to encourage her, cheer her, maybe offer to go with her to church so she could find out what she needed to know.

But again it was Abby who gave to him, who helped him. He owed her a lot.

"I'm finished." She leaned back from her table, stretched her back and laid down her instrument. "I can't work any more. I've got to move or I'll never walk again."

"Oh." Donovan's watch read ten-thirty. "Wow! I had no idea." He rose, shuffled the stack of papers together. "I should have gone home ages ago."

"Who's watching Ariane?"

He grinned, delighted with his news.

"She's on a sleepover at Jessica's."

"You're kidding. That's progress." Abby locked the safe, pulled on her jacket. "Whose idea was that?"

"Jessica's. She is adamant that she'll be the first one Ari has over in her new room."

"That's good, Donovan. It means Ariane is willing to try things. Has she said anything yet?"

He shook his head.

"Well, I'm sure she will soon. Every day she's accepting her new life a little more."

"Yeah." He raced to leave his drawings on his own desk while Abby locked her office. They met at the back door. "You said you need to move. You're not going walking at this time of night, are you?"

Abby's love of walking had worn him out many times.

"Why not? My neighborhood is safe." She buttoned her jacket. "I need to get some exercise or I'll end up planted to that chair."

"What if I walk with you?" He rattled the keys in his pocket. "The real estate agent dropped off the keys to Heritage House today. Officially I don't take over until next week, but the sellers okayed it and she didn't see any reason I couldn't get it early to measure and stuff."

"You want to walk around Heritage House?" Abby shrugged. "I suppose those grounds are as good as any. You can get a feel for your yard at night and I'll protect you from the boogey men."

"Yeah," he agreed, studying her five-foot-five frame and small delicate hands. "You're big protection."

"Boo!" she yelled. He flinched backward. "Don't knock me, Don."

Donovan had to laugh as he followed her to Heritage House. What a girl. She got down but she picked herself up. She had questions, so she made up her mind to find answers. She needed a design theme, so she found one that would make senior marketers green with envy, and in the process she came up with a blockbuster concept for her own department.

He'd known her for years, yet Abby still stunned him with her abilities.

But Donovan had a sense that tonight she wouldn't be as free with her inner thoughts. There was something new about her, a barrier she'd erected that he couldn't breach, wasn't sure he should try.

Abby wasn't a schoolgirl anymore. He kept forgetting that. In his mind he kept relegating her to the shy, repressed teen he'd known five years ago. But just as he'd changed, Abby had become someone different.

Abby Franklin was a woman who was serious about her goals and wasn't playing games with her life.

If he'd expected Abby to be his playmate, Donovan realized now that it wasn't going to happen. She was willing to give, but Abby had her own needs, her own goals. And they deserved fulfilling every bit as much as his did. Maybe it was time for him to give back.

And that scared him more than anything he'd taken on so far.

Because if they moved from pals, buddies, to something more, he knew he'd fail her.

And failure to be the kind of friend she needed would hurt Abby. Maybe more now than ever.

"But what else can I do, Lord? I can't walk away. She's a seeker, asking questions, wanting to know you. I have to help however I can."

As he drove, Donovan prayed for wisdom and guidance, for the grace to know when to back off and when to speak. When he finally pulled into the driveway of Heritage House, he shut off the motor and closed his eyes, grateful for the few minutes Abby would need to catch up. Funny how he'd come to depend on these quick minutes of conversation with God.

"Are you intending to sit there for the whole walk?" Abby demanded as she opened his door. Wind tore at her hair, billowing her jacket, spinning the leaves above them in some mad dance of night.

"You didn't choose a very good time to walk. Are you sure

you—okay. Okay." He let her pull his arm and left the safety of the car. "Those look like storm clouds."

"I love storm clouds. They're invigorating. Challenging. They chase away the cobwebs." She slid her arm through his elbow and began walking up the drive, her steps light and fast. "Behold your kingdom, Donovan."

A few minutes of pacing along beside her and he, too, began to feel brighter, excited.

"I can't believe all the ideas I got from you tonight. You should be charging Woodwards."

"That's silly. Woodwards is my inspiration. So is this place. Imagine a birthday party on the front lawn, Don. Kids racing all over. A stack of presents a mile high. Or no." She clapped a hand to her mouth. "Imagine putting a tent out here. Sleeping outside on this big lovely lawn."

Abby twirled around and tripped over her own feet, tumbling to the ground. Donovan offered her a hand up, but she simply sat there laughing up at him, her eyes glinting with merriment.

"What if you had a son, Don? A little boy who loved to climb trees. Wouldn't this be the perfect place for him? That old oak is just begging to be climbed."

"What about at Christmas," he said, catching her spirit. "Imagine the fun you could have with lights. A manger scene there, right where we first saw the house. Those two spruce boughs make a perfect frame. I'll have lights on the house, of course. Lots of them. Dad will help. He's nuts for Christmas lights."

"Snow dusting the drive. Smells of cinnamon and berry pies wafting out whenever the door opens. People stopping by, carolers. Sliding over this slope on a toboggan." Abby lay back on the grass and studied a huge pine. "There's your Christmas tree."

Donovan sat down beside her, studying her rather than the land. "New Year's parties, spring egg hunts, Fourth of July.

Thanksgiving with a ton of pumpkins." He grinned at her. "I'm really doing this, Abby."

"You really are," she murmured. "I'm so proud of you, Don."

"Thanks. You're still coming with us on Saturday, aren't you?"

"Saturday? Oh, the furniture." A tiny frown creased the corners of her eyes. "Yes, I'll go." She rose. "We're supposed to be walking."

"You don't sound thrilled about spending my money." He dropped the teasing note when she didn't respond. "What's wrong?"

"Nothing. I have to stay at Mom's Friday night with Dad. She's going to some Bible study." Abby resumed her speed walk.

"That's good, isn't it?" He matched her pace, enjoying the wind against his face, the smell of rain about to burst out of the clouds, the fresh aroma of pine needles.

"Yes, it's good. And I do need to spend more time with Dad. I wish I could get him interested in something all his own. Sometimes I feel like she resents him and I think Dad feels it, too."

"What does he like to do?"

"I don't think he's ever had enough time to figure that out." Abby giggled as he marched to the front door, turned and began pacing back down the drive. "It's scary to think about getting old, isn't it?"

"Is it?" Donovan felt a splash against his cheek and ignored it. He wasn't giving up this time with Abby.

"Haven't you ever thought about the future, Donovan?"

He made a face at her and she giggled.

"Yeah, dumb question."

"What do you see in your future, Abby?"

"Winning the contest?"

"Of course. But what else?" Donovan waited then pressed. "Marriage? Kids?"

She was silent for a long time. In fact, they reached the car before she finally spoke.

"I don't look too far into the future anymore."

"Why not?"

"The present is enough for me to deal with, I guess. If I can get to New York, I'll be happy." She inclined her head toward the pavement. "Ready?"

"Again?" he groaned as she picked up her pace. "I'll never get out of bed tomorrow morning."

"This will get you into shape. Prepare you for the labor of house-owning."

"You're a very scary person, for someone so small." He grabbed her hand and held it as they climbed the drive once more.

"I wonder if animals would be good for Dad."

"You're going to get him a dog?"

Abby sniffed. "My mother would not allow an animal in the house."

"Hmm. It's a good idea, though." In fact, Donovan imagined Mark would flourish around animals. Maybe this was something he could help Abby with. He'd have to give it some thought.

They walked in companionable silence until thunder echoed down the streets.

"One thousand three, one thousand four." Donovan counted it out as he had when he was a child.

Way in the distance, lightning speared the black velvet cloak of night.

"Closer than I thought. We'd better get home before we get soaked."

Abby grunted her agreement but stood staring at the house.

"Soon you will be home when you come here," she whispered. "You can run inside and shut the door and be safe in your own little sanctuary."

A note of deep longing underlay her words. At least Donovan thought it was longing. But he also heard loneliness combined with sadness. He didn't know what to say to alleviate it. He didn't know how to help her, so he did the only thing he was good at. He wrapped his arm around her shoulder, drew her against his side and offered, "Coffee?" in a bright cheery voice.

Abby shook her head, eased out from under his arm.

"Thanks, Don. But it's late and I should get home."

The bubbling vivacity that she'd radiated earlier had drained away. The bounce in her step, the sparkle in her eyes, the stalwart facing forward into the wind—all of it had dissipated into the night. Now Abby looked small and lonely.

And he wanted to protect her, care for her.

"Goodnight, Donovan. See you tomorrow." She waggled her fingers at him, then walked to her car.

"Goodnight, Abby."

A moment later the darkness swallowed up her little car and he was alone.

Donovan fiddled with the house keys for less than three seconds before he made up his mind and let himself into Heritage House. The security code was easily entered. Then he moved from room to room, switching on lights as he went until the house was ablaze.

He moved to the sunroom. Across the darkness of the yard, the sky flashed and blazed as the storm moved in. He had no idea how long he stood there watching, only that the glory and majesty of the heavens could not erase the image of Abby's pensive face.

"This is the right move for me, Father. I know that you ordained it and that you will bless us in this house. But, oh Lord, what am I to do about Abby?"

He couldn't speak the words, couldn't say how much he wanted to fix Abby's world, to give her the things she'd never had, to reassure her that she was loved.

But Donovan had a sense that God knew that deep inside his heart, Abigail Franklin had taken root. In fact, he'd begun to wonder if she'd ever left.

So…did you call that love?

Chapter Eleven

"I think I liked spending your money."

"Well, get over it because there's none left. I'm going to be bound to this house for the rest of my life."

"Lucky you." Abby smiled at Donovan before turning her focus on the delivery men who were parading in and out of Heritage House with all the furniture she, Donovan and Ariane had purchased a few weeks earlier.

"Ariane," she called, when the first piece that belonged to a white four-poster set came through the door.

Ariane scampered in.

"Here's your stuff. Why don't you show the men where it goes?"

After performing a little twirl of ecstasy, Ariane raced up the stairs.

"She wants to talk, I know it. But she won't." Donovan's face wore a troubled look. "Olivia says it might take something big to make her finally let go of the last barriers."

"Olivia would know. She's the child psychologist." Abby pointed to the dining room where the men deposited a long sleek dining table. "Aren't you glad you went with me on that table? It couldn't fit better."

"It's pretty good. In fact, the whole house is looking great. Thanks to you."

"And a big store. And your credit card."

"Don't remind me." He rubbed his flat stomach. "I'm starving."

"If the phone's working, you could order a pizza. The delivery men are almost finished unloading anyway."

While Donovan busied himself with acquiring nourishment, Abby concentrated on getting the last piece, Ariane's piano, into the family room. She couldn't be happier about how the room looked. It had exceeded even her expectations.

"Except for that horrid chair," she muttered, glaring at the offending black leather recliner that took up as much space as a hospital bed. Maybe Donovan would see how awful it was and get the delivery men to take it back.

"Don't touch that!" Donovan flopped into it and extended the footrest until it had reached its maximum. "I love this chair. Perfect for story times and paper reading and musing on wintry nights."

"Musing?" Abby rolled her eyes. "For my dad, maybe."

"Speaking of whom—how's he doing?"

"You saw him when you stopped by last Friday night. How did he seem to you?"

"Bored. I have an idea about that."

But before Donovan could say more, the delivery men announced they were finished and the pizza arrived. Donovan lit a fire in the hearth and spread a quilt on the hardwood floor. When he brought in paper cups and a jug of chocolate milk, Abby frowned.

"Chocolate?"

"It's a house, Abby. Not a museum. It's the family that lives here who matter, not the things. If something spills, we'll clean it up."

"You're right."

The family. Did that mean he considered her a part of his family?

Ariane rushed down the stairs at Donovan's call, panting and pink-cheeked.

"Your room's all set?" Donovan asked. Ariane nodded eagerly. "Be sure because you're sleeping in there tonight. I don't want you to wake me up at three o'clock in the morning to tell me those guys forgot to bring your mattress."

He tickled her under the chin. Ariane's response made Abby teary-eyed.

"Speak," she wanted to say. "Just let it out."

But even though Ariane opened her lips several times, no words emerged.

"This pizza is getting cold," Abby murmured. She and Donovan shared a look before he began laying pieces on paper plates.

Fortunately, there were no spills and the "dishes" were quickly disposed of. Earlier, Abby had loaded all the new dishes, cutlery and glassware into the dishwasher. It took her and Ariane only a few minutes to unload it and stock the cupboards. By then, Donovan had disappeared.

They found him in the garage.

"Oh, no. You're not spending the evening under the hood of your car, are you?" Disappointment filled Abby.

"Why not? I'm sure you girls have lots to explore." He studied Ariane. "Swimming? I guess you could. I had the pool checked out yesterday. Everything's good. Want to swim?" he asked Abby.

"Me?" Abby frowned. She'd offered to help because she wanted to make sure they were comfortable, to help Donovan find his feet. "I can't. I have to go."

The words tumbled out in a rush, unbelievable and rather silly.

"It's Thursday. You don't have to go to your parents and make dinner or stay with your dad. You said you were free tonight."

Free—to be with you.

Abby debated a moment before she asked Ariane to go inside. She should stifle her criticism, but Donovan was her friend and she was concerned about Ariane. She had to say something.

"Are you going to make this a habit?" she asked quietly when they were alone.

"What?"

"Doing what needs to be done then running away."

"I'm not doing that." His blue eyes hardened.

"You're not playing with Ariane, either. She needs time with you, Donovan. Not time when you're overseeing furniture arrivals or time when your attention and focus is divided between her and something else. She needs time with *you*. I can't take your place."

He frowned.

"I guess it is a school night, not ideal for swimming."

"It's not about the night or the activity. Ariane needs to know you are going to make time for her. You and she, together."

"You push hard, Abby." He closed the hood with a sigh. "What's worse, you're right. I keep forgetting it's not just me in my world anymore. Come on, I sense a game of Chinese checkers coming on."

They played several games, laughing and teasing each other. Just like a family.

But she wasn't part of this family. The thought stabbed Abby so hard she was glad when Ariane yawned and Donovan decreed bedtime had arrived.

"I must go now. Thanks for the pizza and the game." She kissed Ariane and received a hug in return. "Enjoy your new house, honey. I hope you'll be very happy here."

They walked her to the door.

"I can't tell you how much I appreciate your help, Abby."

"My pleasure." She wasn't going to prolong this. It already hurt that she had to leave. What about when she moved permanently? "Enjoy your home, Donovan. Goodnight."

He caught her arm before she could escape.

"Don't I get a hug?" he teased.

It took every ounce of internal fortitude Abby had to wrap her arms around him. He hugged her close, obviously unaware of the turmoil she experienced. The poignancy of the moment heightened when memories of a night five years ago swamped her. She pushed away the fog of yearning and eased away from him.

"Bye." She swung away out the door and did not look back, even when Donovan called goodnight.

In the sanctity of her car, Abby let the tears drip down her cheeks. She shifted into gear and pulled out of his parking space, onto his driveway and rolled off of his property.

She drove straight home. Inside her small apartment, Abby did not flick on the lights. Instead she went to the French doors that offered a view of downtown Denver, backlit by the purplish glow of the sunset beyond the craggy mountain peaks.

And there she faced the truth.

The feelings she had for Donovan Woodward five years ago had never died. She wasn't going her own way, building her own life with nary a thought about him. The past wasn't, as she'd insisted to Donovan, over. The flames of the past had not been doused but merely banked.

Abby still loved him, though differently than she had before.

But that way lay futility. Donovan had high expectations of his world, but there was no indication that he expected Abby to be in it as anything more than a friend. And after tonight, Abby knew she wanted way more than friendship.

She wanted honest, true love that withstood the storms and pushed ahead to a future of promise. She wanted the knowledge that someone had her back, that she could count on Donovan whenever the need arose.

That longing had lain in her heart ever since she'd been a teen. Abby accepted that her parents couldn't fill that role.

Donovan had proven he couldn't by running away. So why did these feelings persist?

The Bible she was using for her group study lay on a table nearby. Abby picked it up, held it to her chest and prayed.

"I'm trying to understand what you require of me, who I need to be. But I don't understand this. Please erase him from my heart. Focus my attention on the contest."

Abby prayed the same prayer over and over, in different versions.

But by midnight, she did not feel the inner assurance her study book talked about. She didn't even feel that God had heard her.

"Faith," she told herself. "Remember that it all happens by faith. The Bible says he hears us, so he does."

It was the only thing Abby had to cling to.

Fridays were never smooth at Weddings by Woodwards. This one was a culmination of the perfect storm.

Donovan had been put in charge of the kitchens. "That's Katie's forte," he protested.

Taking responsibility, doing his best, that was God's will for him and Donovan was cool with that. But cooking?

"Katie's out, probably for the week." His beautiful mother had never looked more flustered. "She's got some bug, the doctor says."

"Sara?"

"Is taking over in other areas. Your father and I are doing as much as we can. Since Winifred had to go to Chicago, we're really strapped. We're expecting you to pull your weight, Donovan."

The way she said it, the hesitation behind the words told him she wouldn't be surprised if he backed out. How often had he disappointed them?

"Of course I'll help. Tell me what you need." He listened, aghast, as she explained the kitchen shortage. "But, Mom, I know nothing about cooking! What good can I do there?"

"Figure it out. I have to go prepare for that candlelight wedding tonight." She kissed his forehead. "Remember, you can ask for God's help. You'll do fine."

"Yeah." He watched her walk away and knew suddenly exactly how Ariane must feel sometimes. "Okay, God. Now what?"

"Talking to yourself?" Abby asked, entering the room.

Donovan filled her in on the catastrophe in the making. "I'm assigned the kitchens."

"There goes our reputation." Her eyes danced although she didn't laugh at him outright.

"Abby?"

They both whirled to see Mary, hands knotted around her soft calfskin bag.

"Oh, hi, Mom. What are you doing here?"

"Some colleagues of your father are treating him to lunch and the movies, so I'm having a day of luxury. I stopped by to see if you are free for lunch."

Donovan found a crack of light in his otherwise bleak day. He'd been going to arrange something with her mother anyway, to help Abby. Now he didn't have to figure out how to pull it together.

"Mrs. Franklin, are you still interested in French cooking?"

"Of course. Why do you ask?"

"It so happens we are in desperate need of help in the kitchen. That wedding food you sampled a few weeks ago is on the menu tonight and our chef could really use an extra pair of hands. Is that something you'd be interested in?"

Abby stared at him, mouth open and eyes wide. But Donovan was pretty sure this was the right move.

"Well, I've never actually cooked—"

"Doesn't matter. Chef will show you the ropes. Interested?"

"Yes." Mary began unbuttoning her jacket. "Where should I start?"

"I'll show you." Donovan escorted her toward the kitchen,

glancing back over one shoulder to grin at Abby, who still looked dazed.

The rest of the day passed in such a flurry of activity that when Donovan felt tiny fingers touch his arm, he jerked back, shocked to see Ariane standing next to him in the workroom of his father's floral area.

"Are you back from school already?" he asked, checking his watch.

She pointed to the flower petals he was pulling from wilted roses.

"The flower girl will drop these in front of the bride when she walks down the aisle," he explained. She feathered one fingertip across the delicate petals. "You want to help?"

With an eager nod she picked up a rose and with skill and precision removed each petal.

"You're better at this than I am."

Ariane climbed onto a stool beside him and worked silently. He'd never get a better chance.

"Ari, why won't you talk? Did I do something wrong?"

She shook her head, her dark brown eyes still holding that wistfulness that never quite disappeared.

"You're okay about the house?"

This brought an eager response.

"Then why, Ari? It's not good for you to keep silent. I worry when you won't tell me why." Donovan opened his heart. "It makes me feel I'm not doing a good job looking after you. If your dad saw you so sad, I think he'd be very angry at me."

She dropped her rose and threw her arms around his neck, hugging him so tightly, Donovan felt his heart jerk to a halt. After a few moments, Ari pulled away. She drew a heart in midair and pointed to him.

"I love you, too, sweetie. That's why it hurts so much when you won't speak to me."

Tears puddled on her cheeks as she stared at him.

"Oh, don't cry. You don't have to talk if you don't want to." He pulled her into his arms and held her, wishing he was better at this fatherhood business. "It's okay. I only want to help you."

Ari seemed content to rest there for a while, her head tucked against his chest.

"I wish you'd talk to me," he told her quietly. "I miss your dad. I'd like to share some of my memories with you. And you could share yours with me. I don't want us ever to forget him."

Ari drew back, studied his face and finally nodded.

"We'll do that, okay? Someday?"

She nodded and smiled. A moment later she was back on her stool concentrating on the rose petals.

"Well, don't you two look cute?" Abby leaned against the doorframe, her hazel gaze pensive. "Need some help?"

Ari nodded.

"Sure." Donovan dragged over another stool. "This is my absolute last job for this wedding. I think."

"I know the feeling. I've been helping bridesmaids into their dresses for the last half hour. I am so not cut out for that job." She plopped down on the stool and began plucking rose petals with a fierceness that made Donovan laugh.

"What happened?"

"I always thought the wedding was about the bride and groom, but those ladies are so self-centered I wouldn't put it past them to completely upstage the bride." Abby hopped off the stool. "'She should have chosen a different color. This fades my eyes.' 'This fabric is really not top quality silk.' 'Woodwards made a mistake with my fitting. My dress is too tight.'" Abby accompanied each comment with a pantomime that made Ari giggle. "There was nothing wrong with any of those gowns. It was the person in them."

"Sounds like a fun time."

"A riot," she grumbled. "How's Mom doing?"

"Oh." Donovan gulped. "I completely forgot about her.

We've done enough of these." He helped Ari off the stool and offered a hand to Abby. "We'd better go check on her. Chef gets into a bit of a temper when things aren't going well."

Talk about a vast understatement. If Mary and Chef were at war, the onus of any failure in the kitchen would land squarely on Donovan's shoulders. And not just from his family. Mary would use it against him, too, he was certain.

On the way to the kitchen, Donovan couldn't help admiring Abby's suit. She tended to choose jewel tones. Today it was sea-deep aquamarine that reminded him of diving in the Mediterranean. The color suited her even though she'd lost some of her impeccable style—no doubt the aftermath of the bickering bridesmaids.

"Let me go first," he advised them, holding a hand to bar entry to the kitchen. "If it's bad, you two might as well escape while you can."

But when he pushed the door open, all Donovan could hear was two voices in quiet conversation. He stepped inside and blinked. Mary and Chef were seated at a table, drinking tea as they talked. Before he could back out, Chef saw him.

"Donovan! Thank you for the gift."

"Uh, you're welcome." He held the door open for Abby and Ari, while wondering what he'd done this time.

"Mary is a marvelous assistant. She knows exactly what to do and stands up to me when I try to boss her." He grinned as if this was a good thing.

"I must thank you, too, Donovan," Mary said, her eyes bright and smile wide with pleasure. "This has been the most fun I've had in ages."

Thank him? Donovan gulped, shot a glance Abby's way. She looked like a deer caught in the headlights, too. He winced, knowing he should have told her his suspicions before this.

"You enjoy the kitchen, Mom?"

"It's wonderful. The dishes are specially tailored for each

occasion, you know. Chef's been telling me how he decides on them." Mary held up a piece of paper. "I've been writing down some recipes."

As far as Donovan knew, Chef kept every recipe a closely guarded secret. Mary *had* made an impression.

"We are sampling leftovers from the wedding cake. Care to join us?" Chef held up a massive teapot.

"But—the reception?" Donovan checked his watch. "It's not that far off. Don't you have to—" get going, was what he wanted to say. But one did not push Chef.

"Everything is under control. The helpers are taking a break. In ten minutes we'll head for the finish line." With a jovial laugh he poured all of them a cup of tea, even Ariane to which he added a huge dollop of milk.

"The tea is great but this cake—it's fantastic."

"Abby loves anything with lime," Mary interjected.

Donovan couldn't remember a time when he'd seen this mother bestow such a tender glance on her daughter. They chatted and ate until Abby's question about her father brought back reality.

"Mom, these friends of Dad, are they taking him home or do you have to pick him up?"

"Mercy, I forgot all about. I'm to meet them at the mall." Mary jumped up, then looked at Chef with a troubled face. "Is it all right for me to leave now?" she asked with great deference. "It won't put you in a jam?"

"You've done a wonderful job of getting us out of the jam." Chef grasped her hands and kissed her cheek. "If ever you wish a part-time job, please tell Donovan. I would have you back here in a minute and there are not a lot of people I say that about."

"Thank you very much. I've enjoyed myself." Mary pulled on her jacket. "I'll have to talk to Mark about it. I don't see how it can work, but I will think it over."

"Good."

Mary turned to Donovan, her manner cooling.

"Donovan, shall I take Ariane with me? I could start her lesson as soon as we get home."

"Good idea. I'll pick her up at the usual time."

"Perhaps you'll stay for dinner?" she offered quietly. "I'm sure whatever Abby's making will be delicious."

Donovan felt more than saw Abby jerk upright at the mention of dinner.

"I'd love to stay for dinner, if it's all right with Abby."

"It's fine." Abby looked dazed.

Donovan saw the older woman and the young girl off, then returned to his office. Abby sat in wait.

"What is going on?"

"I don't know what you mean."

"My mother. Inviting you for dinner. Cooking, and loving it. Since when? And why aren't you surprised?"

"I had a hunch she was only pretending about the cooking thing the day we brought them lunch. She asked so many intelligent questions. Someone who hates cooking wouldn't care to know, but she wanted details." He met her glare sheepishly. "I was trying to come up with a way to get her in here. God worked it all out."

"God did?" Skepticism laced Abby's voice.

"Yep." He grinned. "Have you ever seen your mom in the kitchens before?"

"No. Never."

"Then?" He lifted one eyebrow.

"God. You think?"

He nodded.

"Well, I'm glad she has a new interest."

"I'm not sure it is a new interest. But I'm fairly certain the reason she has you making dinner on Friday nights is not because she doesn't like cooking."

Abby curled up her nose. "It isn't?"

"I think that's how Mary ensures her daughter will come to visit."

"Oh." She thought about it a moment, then nodded. "Makes sense, I guess, in a weird way. But I'm a little concerned that pursuing her interest will make Dad feel like he's in the way."

"Just have to pray about it," Donovan said as an idea began brewing in the back of his mind.

"There's an awful lot to pray about, isn't there?" Abby didn't meet his eyes. "I've been reading scriptures on prayer. There are tons of them."

"But it doesn't have to be hard," he said, glad Abby was reading the Bible so intently. "After all, prayer is conversation and we humans are usually good at that."

Abby studied him for several moments. Finally she spoke. "Can I ask you something?"

"Why not?"

"It's kind of personal."

"Shoot. If I can't answer, I won't."

"What do you pray for, Donovan?"

He thought about it for a minute. "Mostly wisdom to make the right decisions, I guess."

"Not things you want?"

"Well, I ask God to bless my plans and help me to honor him." He frowned, concerned by her questions. "Why are you asking?"

"I really thought I understood what God wanted from me. To be a good daughter, to work as hard as I can for Woodwards, even to do well in the contest."

"And now you're not so sure about the contest," he guessed.

"No. Because try as I might, things just aren't coming together. I can't get enough time, for one thing. And I think I'm going to have trouble financing the jewels for a couple of pieces."

"Do you need a loan? I could ask Grandmother—"

She shook her head vehemently.

"No. This is my baby. I need to manage on my own."

"Why? You used Art's money. Why can't anyone else help?" She was being stubborn. Frustrated, Donovan lashed out, "Why can't you accept help from my family? What's wrong with us that you'd rather give up than ask my grandmother?"

"Because I need the satisfaction of doing this alone."

"To prove to your mother. Did it ever occur to you, Abby, that maybe God put you in this situation so you would turn to other people and let them help?"

"God did?" She looked as if her best friend had betrayed her. "No, Don. I can honestly say I never thought of that." She got to her feet. "I need to get back to work. I'll see you at my parents' condo later."

His heart aching to ease her pain, Donovan watched her leave. He replayed the scene over and over in his mind, wishing he'd handled it better. But then he realized that Abby hadn't told him everything. She'd used her mother as an excuse because there was something else underlying her concerns. Something she wouldn't or couldn't share with him.

Donovan prayed about it for a while, wishing he could find a way to change things because when Abby hurt, he hurt.

"Please, please don't let Abby lose out on this opportunity. Be with her, guide her. And help me to be there if she needs me." He thought a moment longer and added, "Help her to need me. She needs to know I won't run away again."

Donovan tidied up his desk. He ensured everything for the evening wedding was in hand, then he grabbed his keys and headed for the Franklins' home. Now that he had his own home, he'd invite them to his place for dinner.

As soon as he learned how to make dinner.

Or when Abby offered. It was getting so Abby figured into a lot of his decisions.

What would he do when she was gone?

Chapter Twelve

"I don't want to harp, but I'll need to know really soon, Mom."

"Why the sudden rush for this money?"

"I've got to get the gems and size them before I can place them in my designs." Abby spread grated cheese over her spaghetti casserole and set it in the oven to bake.

"I've said I'll talk to your father, Abby. And I will. But don't be too hopeful. Most of our money is tied up, as you know." Mary went to set the table. When she returned, she spoke in an almost whisper. "Besides, I don't approve of your work."

"I know. You've told me many times. But it is what I've chosen to do." Abby wanted to say more, to remind her mother how wonderful she'd felt discovering her own dream. But she had no chance because Donovan arrived. Her heart gave a bump at his handsome face and the smile he sent her way.

"Hi. Am I late?"

"No." Mary pulled him into the living room. "Listen to Ari's newest song."

Abby stood in the background, listening as a part of her brain marveled at her mother's lack of faith in her. How could losing her dream be part of God's love?

It was all too painful and confusing.

"Dinnertime."

The spaghetti disappeared in record time. Conversation flowed easily as Mary described her day at Weddings by Woodwards. Not to be outdone, Mark told them of his afternoon. Later Donovan insisted he be allowed to help Abby clean up.

"The due date for those designs is a week from today, isn't it?"

Abby nodded, pretending great involvement in scrubbing the casserole dish.

"Are you ready?"

"No. But it doesn't matter."

He took the scrub brush out of her hand and tilted her chin so she was forced to look at him.

"What's wrong?"

"My mother promised to lend me the money to buy some gems for two pieces. I think she's going to back out."

"What? But that's—"

"The way it is." She shook her head when he would have protested and added another dollop of lemon-scented soap to her water. "It doesn't matter anyway. I haven't had time to complete the metal work. I just can't seem to fit everything into my schedule."

"Actually, I had an idea about that." Donovan poured soap into the dishwasher cup, then started the machine. "Ari has been bugging me about getting a dog. But she's never been around animals, so I made an appointment for us to visit the animal shelter tonight."

"That was a good idea," she praised.

"I'm learning." He bowed at the waist, grinned and continued. "Anyway, I wondered if we could take your dad. If I remember rightly, he used to love animals."

"Still does." Abby tipped her head sideways, trying to assess whether Donovan really wanted to do this. "I guess you could ask him."

Donovan grinned at her, then marched into the living room

and posed his question. Mary's reluctance was overridden by Mark's enthusiasm.

"It's a program they have where you can play with the animals, walk them and give them some personal attention that they miss at the shelter."

"I'd love that. When do we leave?" He turned to his wife. "It doesn't matter to you, does it? You have your Bible study and Abby doesn't want to babysit me."

They'd all assumed he hadn't realized, but clearly her father hadn't yet lost all his acuity.

"I love visiting with you, but if you'd rather pet some mangy old dog—" Abby said.

Mark grinned. "Actually I would, dear."

"Well!" Abby huffed, pretending indignation.

"In that case, let's go." Donovan winked at her. "You're welcome to come, too."

"The pity invitation. Thanks, but no thanks. You guys go and have fun."

Donovan arranged a return time when Mary would be home. Then he, Ari and Mark left. Abby grabbed her purse and headed for the door, but her mother stopped her.

"Abby, I've thought about this quite carefully and I do not feel your father and I can lend you the money you asked for. It isn't because we don't believe in you," she said hastily.

"Right." Abby grasped the doorknob, forcing herself to act normally. "Thanks anyway, Mom. I've got to go. Enjoy your Bible study."

Although her mother called to her, Abby ignored her. She scurried away as quickly as she could, barely noticing the cooling evening breeze. Inside she burned with anger.

So this was it. It was over. All that work for nothing.

She got in her car and drove aimlessly as twilight gave way to darkness.

"Why?" was the only word she could manage and she sent it heavenward.

But no answer came.

With a rush of anger she steered the car toward Woodwards. Once inside the building she headed for her office. She pulled each piece from her tiny safe and set it on her desk.

It was good work. But the blank holes were only gaping reminders of how close she'd come.

"Abby? My word, you're working late."

"Hello, Winifred." Abby stayed seated when the older woman stepped forward and bent to examine each piece.

"These are stunning, dear. But where are the gems?"

"I don't have them yet."

"Well, when you get them in, your work will astound your contest judges."

"Thanks." She would not tell Winifred about not having the money to buy the gems and have her rush to the rescue, even if it was allowed.

"You seem troubled, dear. Is everything all right?" Winifred's soft lavender fragrance filled the room. "Can I help?"

"No. But thank you."

"Then I'll pray for you." Winifred must have sensed Abby wanted to be alone for she laid one gentle hand on Abby's head, then sighed. "Goodnight, dear."

"Goodnight."

Abby sat alone in the big empty building, yearning for something that would ease the pain.

But what could heal the knowledge that her own mother didn't think she was capable of winning this contest?

"Abby?" Donovan poked his head around the door. "What are you doing here?"

"Working. Where's Ariane?"

"Ah, I didn't tell you my good news." He moved inside the

room, his swagger pronounced. "I hired a housekeeper/nanny. Her name is Mrs. Beasley and she's the best thing since sliced bread."

"Trying to avoid one-on-one time with Ari, Don?" Abby snapped.

"Nope. Trying to give her the best possible life."

"By hiring someone to take over for you?" Why couldn't he understand that Ariane's insecurity was what kept her silent.

"No, Abby. That's not what I'm doing."

"Then what? She needs love and time with you, Don."

"Which she is getting and will continue to get. But this way she doesn't have to wait at Woodwards for me to finish working, she can go home, run free and maybe have a friend over. And trust me, Mrs. Beasley is the kind of woman who will make Ari feel very loved and cherished." He frowned. "What's wrong with you?"

"Nothing."

"Not true." He shook his head. "You look—I don't know. Squashed."

"That's how I feel." She couldn't look at him. "My mother refuses to lend the money she'd promised."

"Oh, Abby." He drew her into his arms and held her, cheek pressed against his shirtfront. "I'm so sorry."

She slid her arms around his waist, relieved to finally be able to let go of her stiff upper lip and release her emotions.

"What's wrong with me, Don? Why doesn't she love me the way she loves Ariane?"

"She does, Abby. She just doesn't know how to show it." His breath ruffled her hair. "Mary is living in fear. Your father's disease, their changed circumstances, their retirement—everything is probably worlds away from what she imagined. And she has no control over any of it. That makes her scared to reach out."

"You're talking about recently." It felt so wonderful to share this with Don. He, of all people, knew how alone she felt. "I'm talking about my whole life."

"So am I." He eased her away so he could see her face. "Your father told me something tonight while we were at the shelter that might put all of this into perspective."

"Oh, yeah?" She stared up at him, wondering what he meant.

"Yeah. Your dad said they tried to have you for many years and that Mary lost three babies. That made her very fearful when she became pregnant with you. The entire pregnancy and all of your early years were filled with worry for her. Eventually she received treatment for anxiety disorder, but I don't think she ever fully recovered."

"They never told me that." Abby blinked, trying to imagine her strong, confident mother worrying about anything.

"Apparently she's managed to control it all these years, but your father feels she's never really gotten over her fear of what might happen."

"I'm—shocked," Abby admitted as she struggled to absorb it.

"So was I. Your dad is a very bright man. He knows what's going to happen to him, but he's determined to spend as much time as he can with your mom. He said her Bible study was helping her deal with her fear."

"The Bible. Isn't it funny how it's impacted all of us." She drew away from him and felt a chill take the place of his warm arms.

"Still having trouble trusting God, Abby?"

"Well, he doesn't seem to help when I ask."

"How do you know? Maybe right now God has something in the works that you can't imagine." He glared at her sternly. "That's why you must not give up."

"Donovan, I have no stones for these pieces."

"Yet."

A note of hope laced the undertones of his voice.

"Do you know something I don't?" she murmured, afraid to believe and yet longing to. "What aren't you saying, Donovan?"

"I don't know anything except that God is the giver of dreams. His imaginings go far beyond anything we can ask or think." Donovan brushed her cheek with his palm, then let his hand rest on her shoulder. "The only thing I know for sure, Abby, is that I can put my faith in God and let him take care of the details."

"You're that sure of God?"

He nodded, blue eyes blazing.

"You want to talk about love, look at God. He personifies love."

Abby thought about it. Finally she nodded and forced a smile to her lips.

"Okay, I'll try to keep trusting. But it isn't easy."

"Come on, it's time for all pretty jewelry designers to go to bed," he said.

Once she'd locked her office, Donovan grasped her hand and led her from the building. When they reached her car, he moved and she was encircled by his arms.

"I'm spending tomorrow morning with Ari and your dad and the animals. Why don't you sleep in and relax? You need to take a break, Abby."

"Boy, I must look awful." She poked her tongue at him.

Donovan laughed and drew her against his heart.

"You look as beautiful as you always have, Abby." He dipped his head and touched her lips.

Even though she wanted to pull him closer and return his embrace, Abby couldn't let herself forget that her goal was to leave Woodwards, Denver and Donovan.

So she stood immobile, savoring the touch of his lips, his warm breath, the way his fingers fiddled with her hair. And when he drew back, she stifled her heart's cry for more.

"You are an awesome woman, Abby Franklin. And I care about you a great deal."

Care about? It wasn't enough. She wanted more. But Donovan wasn't the kind of man for a needy, ordinary person like her. Anyway, it couldn't work out. He'd come home to his family. She wanted to leave.

Abby stepped out of his embrace. She allowed herself one touch to his cheek.

"Thank you for coming, Donovan. Goodnight."

Without saying another word she climbed into her car and drove away.

"Help me," was the only prayer she could offer all the way home.

When Donovan needed answers, after God, Grandmother was his best resource.

Today he waited in her office, unable to relax or get comfortable. He had to do something to help Abby. No way was he going to sit back and watch her dreams go up in flames. She had the designs, the creativity and the ability to carry them off. All she needed was someone to bolster her confidence and offer a little backing.

That would be him. With Grandmother's help.

"Donovan? My word, you're the early bird."

"Same as you, Granny." He used the familiarity deliberately. "Have you got a few minutes for me now?"

"As long as you need." She carried her coffee to one of the soft comfy chairs she adored and beckoned him to join her. "What's wrong?"

"Nothing. I have something to show you."

Donovan took his time laying out the storyboards for her to see the campaign he'd devised for the jewelry department. His grandmother studied the first, then eased forward.

"You're calling it 'Generations'?"

"Yes. It's an idea I took from Abby. Her project for the

contest is called 'Heritage.' It could be easily included in this. In fact, I've used a couple of her designs here. The thrust of 'Generations' is that Weddings by Woodwards isn't just for weddings, but can play a part in the ongoing life of any bride and groom."

Donovan pitched his idea confidently, certain that this direction was one Winifred wanted to pursue. When he was finished he sat down and waited.

"This is a very aggressive campaign. It reaches out progressively from the bride and groom to new parents, mid-lifers, seniors." Winifred rose from her seat and hugged him. "It's a fantastic plan, Donovan. More than I hoped you and Abby would come up with when I assigned you the project. When can we get started?"

"Right away." Vindication at last. Donovan sent grateful thanks heavenward. "Abby had a lot of input on this," he repeated. "If it wasn't for her and her suggestions, I wouldn't have known how to pull it all together."

"How are her contest entries coming?"

Donovan debated whether to tell Winifred, but in the end he decided she, of all people, might have a solution so he told her about the loan that had been refused and how it had decimated Abby.

"Her parents, particularly her mother, don't seem to understand how much her refusal undermines Abby's self-esteem." He related what Mark had told him.

"Which explains a lot, but doesn't make anything any easier," Winifred mused. "Poor Abby."

"More than you know. I think Mary's negativity is killing Abby's dream."

"You sound like you've begun to have feelings for her. Again."

"To be truthful, Grandmother, I'm not sure those feelings ever died," he admitted. "I was a stupid fool back then. I thought only of myself, I never really considered Abby's feelings on anything. I listened to her mother's lies and didn't check with Abby about her plans. I'm pretty sure that was a mistake."

"So what now?"

"I don't know. I wish Abby could trust me enough to confide all her problems, but she thinks I'm the one who ran out on her. Given my actions, she has a reason for her distrust. I can't figure out how to change things."

"Maybe you can't." Winifred returned to her seat and sipped her coffee. "Maybe it's too late for your love."

"It can't be!"

As the words left his lips, Donovan finally admitted what his heart already knew. He cared about Abby Franklin more than he ever had.

"Abby's part of my life, Grandmother. And part of my heart. Heritage House, Woodwards, even this marketing campaign— all of it means very little unless Abby's here." He tried to imagine life without her and blanked. "She's the one who helped me figure out how to connect with Ari. She's a huge part of my past and she's the one I want in my future."

"Why don't you tell her that?"

"She wouldn't believe me." The admission cost him. "I dumped her in the worst possible way, Granny. And even if she did believe me, what could she do? She's wanted to work in New York since forever. I can't, I won't, ask her to give up her dream. Besides, I'm pretty sure Abby feels she can't trust me again."

"Well, then, I guess you'll just have to earn that trust."

"How do I do that?" he demanded. "What thing can I do to make her understand that now and always she and Ari come first in my life? Tell me, Grandmother."

"I can't tell you that, Donovan. I can only say that if Abby is the woman in your heart, when the moment comes to prove yourself, God will show you the steps you have to take."

"Keep waiting on God, is that it?" he said with a touch of chagrin.

"He'll never fail you." Winifred rose, patted his shoulder and then gathered up the storyboards. "I'm going to study these some more. This is wonderful work, Donovan. Better than I could have imagined."

"Thanks." He slumped on the sofa, defeat nipping at his heels. What a fool he'd been to walk away from Abby five years ago.

"Donovan?" Winifred stood at her elegant Victorian desk, her thin face troubled. "Why didn't Abby come to me for a loan to buy whatever she needs?"

"Pride, I suppose. She's trying to prove her worth to her mom. Probably to you and me, too." He rose, walked to the door, knowing his few moments with Winifred were over. But he paused in the doorway. "To Abby, winning this contest is going to make everything in her world right again. I'm afraid that if she doesn't send in her entry she'll feel like a failure, or worse, she'll feel that way if she does send it in and doesn't win."

"What about you? How will you feel if she loses?"

"I don't care if Abby scrubs floors, designs jewelry or sits on her thumbs. I only want her to be happy. Winning the contest would do that, I think, but it would also take her away from here." He shrugged. "This time it's out of my hands."

"Then your only option is to pray."

Donovan smiled at her. "Don't think I haven't been. This is my girl we're talking about."

"Does she know that?" Winifred asked, a smile twitching one corner of her pretty pink lips.

"All in due time, Grandmother."

"Don't take too long," she warned.

Donovan walked back to his office, elated by her reception to his ideas, but torn by conflicting desires to run to Abby's office and open his heart, and equally, to keep his own counsel until he had explicit confirmation from God that it was the right time.

A freshness in all you do.

Keeping his word, being there when it counted, being the man of integrity that God expected him to be, that was as fresh as he could manage.

Surely that would be enough to prove to Abby that he'd changed.

Chapter Thirteen

"Are you busy, Abby?"

"Never too busy for you, Winifred. Come in, please. Coffee?"

"I've gone over my daily quota already, thanks. I suppose you're doing last-minute polishing on those entries. I can't tell you how excited we all are. You have a lot of people rooting for you, Abby."

A lot of people were going to be disappointed then, Abby thought.

"May I see the entries?"

"They're, uh, not quite finished."

"Oh?" Winifred's finely arched left brow tilted. "But you have to send them in quite soon, don't you?"

"Three days." Abby paused, then said, "I'm not sure I will be able to send anything."

"Why is that, dear?" Winifred sat down on the only chair available, her backbone ramrod straight. "Are you having problems with the design part?"

"No, I have that nailed down."

"Then it's the gems you need. Good."

"Good?" Abby repeated, confused by Winifred's bright smile.

"Yes, good. Because I was hoping you might use some of

these stones in your work." She opened her palm, peeled back tissue to expose five pieces of jewelry. "It would give me great pleasure if you found any of these stones suitable, Abby."

"But they're lovely pieces. Heirlooms, I'm guessing?" Abby grabbed her monocle and examined each stone.

"Maybe."

"Then?" Abby waited for an explanation.

"I've never told anyone this." Winifred closed her eyes, heaved a heavy sigh, then spoke softly. "Five years after my husband died, I met a man whom I thought was a prince. He bought me lovely gifts, these," she indicated holding out the jewelry.

"Then you must keep them," Abby protested.

"No. Let me finish. He was loving, generous, polite, and fun—all the things I needed after the struggles I had. The one quality he was missing was integrity. I learned that the day he proposed to me. I found out he was already married." Winifred set the pieces on Abby's desk as if holding them was distasteful.

"I'm so sorry." Abby's heart ached for the older woman.

"I confronted him and he disappeared, without those. I never knew what to do with them, so I tucked them away and tried to forget how easily I'd been duped."

"They're great quality pieces. You could have sold them, used the money for your business."

"It would have come in handy, yes," Winifred agreed, her voice quiet. "But I felt it would be profiting from evil. I couldn't do it. I thought maybe his wife needed them. I tried to locate her, but I never could. Which made me feel even worse."

"Of course."

"But Abby, if the gems were removed and used for a good purpose, I think I might finally be able to put those memories to rest permanently." She leaned forward. "You could even use the metals, if you wanted to. It's up to you."

Abby stared at the bounty she'd been given. Was this God's

doing? She'd been praying so hard to know whether to give up or beg for a loan. Was she finally going to be given the opportunity to reach for her goal?

"If you're absolutely certain this is what you want, Winifred, then I can only say thank you very much." She rose and hugged her boss. "I will use them to the best of my ability."

"That's what I hoped," Winifred murmured as she stepped back. "Lock yourself in here for as long as you need to get those entries done. No Weddings by Woodwards business until you've finished what you've begun."

"Yes, ma'am." Abby smiled as she began pulling out her tools.

Winifred watched for a few moments. Then she studied the storyboards Abby had created for "Heritage."

"You know, it occurs to me that your designs fit very well into Donovan's new campaign."

"He showed you? I didn't know." Something so important and he hadn't told her. A ping of hurt reminded her that he had no obligation to her. But still, they'd worked on it together.

"I think he barely finished it last night. He showed it to me very early this morning. I'm sure you'll be next, as soon as he gets back from Ariane's parents' day at school." Winifred touched her cheek. "Donovan has become a very responsible man. I would never have entrusted the work to him if I wasn't already sure, but he's proven himself over and over in the past few weeks. He's changed a lot."

Abby said nothing, confused by the hint underlying Winifred's voice. What was she trying to say?

"If you need someone to confide in, you couldn't choose better, Abby. Or you can always come to me." Winifred walked to the door where she turned, inclined her head and smiled. "I'll be praying for you."

"Thank you." Abby waited until she'd left, then stared at the work before her. Could she do this? She closed her eyes.

"I need help. Please be with me." She added a verse she'd read this morning. "I can do all things through Christ who strengthens me."

Then she set to work.

Frustration ate at Donovan like battery acid through silk. All day he'd been trying to get a moment alone with Abby, to show her the final draft of their ideas. He needed to see the glow in her eyes and watch her face light up to feed this need that had grown in his heart.

But with Ari's parents' day, he'd run behind and played catch-up all day yesterday. Surely this morning he'd get his chance.

He checked Abby's door. Closed.

Weddings by Woodwards wasn't even open yet so the likelihood of her being with a client was slim. He raised his hand to knock. His knuckles froze midair when the door burst open and a ruffled, wrinkled, ravishing Abby appeared.

"Need a coffee?" He held out a cup of her favorite brew.

"You are a genius." She took the cup and drank deeply. "Nectar." She closed her eyes, waiting for the liquid to hit her bloodstream. After a moment her long lashes lifted and her beautiful brown eyes met his. "Thank you."

"No problem." Donovan grinned, held out his own cup. "Need more."

"True sacrifice."

"Anything for you," he said and meant it.

Abby's stare never wavered from his until finally she shook her head.

"No, thank you. This is more than enough. I only wish you'd brought some lemon Danish, too. I'm starved."

"Sorry. No Danish." He noted the lines around her eyes, the mussed up hair, the makeup that had almost disappeared. She had never looked more beautiful to him. "What time did you get in?"

"Yesterday at seven." She beckoned him into her office and flopped into her desk chair.

"You never got any slee—?" The words died on his lips as a sparkle to the right caught his eye. Donovan stepped forward and with great reverence and awe traced one finger over each of the four pieces lying on her desk. "You're finished."

"Do you like them?"

The hesitancy behind those words told Donovan that despite creating these gorgeous things, Abby was still not sure that she was good enough as a designer.

"Like?" He sat in the chair opposite hers. "You know they're spectacular. Don't you?"

She shrugged, slanted her eyes downward. "I like them, but that's no guarantee."

"There are no guarantees in life, Abby. If anyone has learned that, it's me." Because she'd leaned forward to listen, he continued. "You don't always get second chances or the information you need to make the right decision. That's where relying on God comes in."

"Yes," she whispered, her attention fixed on something beyond him, something he couldn't see. "I want so badly to win this, Don. Maybe when I'm finally in New York my mother will see that design is what God wants me to do. Maybe then she'll—"

"She'll what, Abby?" Frustration chewed at Donovan's temper. He was so tempted to blurt Mary's past lies. "Don't set yourself up for more pain. Your mother is never going to accept your work unconditionally. She's spent years and plenty of effort trying to make you into what she wants. She's gone to lengths you can't imagine to retain her dream because it's hard to give up a dream."

"Yes, I know that very well." Abby stared at him in a way he didn't quite understand. He thought he saw hurt, disappointment and perhaps longing all lingering in the shadows of her eyes. Then she blinked it away. "I hear you have some news of your own. Congratulations on the new campaign."

"Thanks." He grinned, his face filled with that wonderful elation once more. "I wanted to show you before I told Grandmother. You were such a big part of it. But I finished the boards only the night before last and either you were busy or I was yesterday. That's why I came in early this morning."

"Good timing." Abby rose, tossed her empty cup into the trash and arched her back. "Let's see it."

After she'd locked her door, he grabbed her hand and drew her toward his office.

"I kind of amplified our Generations idea. Close your eyes." He led her into the center of the room. "Okay, open them."

Abby blinked, then caught her breath. Satisfied with her reaction, Donovan held on to her hand and waited, aware of just how much Abby's opinion mattered to him.

"Fantastic! You've captured the feeling with this. It's perfect." She flung her arms around him and hugged him. "Oh, Donovan, I'm so glad for you."

That embrace, freely given, unstinting and open, was everything he'd longed for and Donovan reveled in it. He slid his arms around her waist and breathed in the faint scent of orange blossoms. With one hand he smoothed away the loose strands from her face so he could study it in the ray of sunshine flooding his window.

"I knew you could do this," she said, eyes shining.

"You did?" He could spend a lifetime studying those eyes.

"Uh-huh. You just had to dig."

"Thank you, Abby." Her lips were millimeters away. Donovan couldn't resist temptation. He bent his head and kissed her, infusing all the things he was afraid to say into his kiss and praying she'd understand.

For a few amazing minutes Abby kissed him back, not as she had five years ago, but with the strength and caring of a woman unafraid to show emotion.

But then she stepped out of his arms.

"It really is great, Donovan." She kept her eyes downcast as she stepped toward the door. "But now I need to get ready for work. See you later?"

"Of course. Abby?"

She paused at the door.

"Yes?"

"I want to come with you to New York." There, he'd said it. "I want to be there to share that success. I want to be your cheering section, if you want. And I want to bring Ari with me."

"Why?" She twisted to stare at him, eyes wide.

"You need a model for the child's bracelet, don't you? Ari could do that. Maybe it would help her." He used the trump card deliberately knowing Abby wouldn't refuse to help a little girl. But it wasn't a lie.

"I don't—"

"She still isn't speaking, Abby. I've tried everything I can think of and she won't say a word. I think it's become a mental thing now, that she won't let herself speak. I'm hoping New York might jolt her out of that."

Abby's full attention was on him now.

"It's gone on too long. She's let go of George, accepted his death and begun to remember him more positively, but still she clings to this silent business. Maybe what I've tried with her has caused more pain, I don't know." He sighed. "I've got to do something to shake her up. You see that, don't you?"

"I know you can't let it go on. But don't beat yourself up, Donovan. You've done your best. And maybe you're right. Maybe in New York she would forget some of her pain and speak. One tiny chink in that armor of hers is all we need." Her smile shared his dilemma. "Okay, come. But be warned, I'll be on pins and needles and not the best company."

"You don't scare me, Abby," he said quietly, holding her gaze. "I know who you are. You can count on me. For anything."

A long silence fell between them while she studied him. Finally she drew a deep breath and nodded.

"Thank you." A second later she was gone.

Donovan sat down and studied his marketing plans. But his mind was on Abby. Surely she understood what he'd implied. Surely she realized that no man kissed a woman the way he had her unless he was serious about that woman.

Didn't she?

Abby shifted in her airplane seat. Understanding Donovan had never been more difficult.

Not that he'd done anything wrong. Far from it. He'd been the consummate host from the moment he picked her up at home, to insisting she take the inside seat on the plane. His conversation was light but interesting. His questions were all about her comfort level. He'd also gone to extreme length to ensure Ariane was also comfortable and relaxed.

But something about him was different.

"The doctor gave me some pills to help make sure she doesn't get sick again like she did when we flew from Paris," he'd told Abby as they boarded the plane. "And I brought a whole bunch of games and her beading kit. Do you think that's enough?"

"Only one way to find out."

They'd taken turns trying to engage Ariane who seemed only to want to sleep. Well, that was understandable given their early morning flight.

"Are you nervous?" Donovan asked.

"I wasn't," Abby drawled, lifting one eyebrow.

"Sorry." He gulped and tried again. "You did get confirmation that your pieces arrived safely?"

Abby turned and glared at him. "You are not helping, Donovan."

"Sorry." He grinned sheepishly. "I think I'm more nervous than anyone."

"You?" She laughed then saw he was serious. "Why?"

"I hope all the judges recognize real talent when they see it, I guess."

He was nervous for her? A sweet hot current headed straight for Abby's heart.

"Plus I've had too much caffeine. And I didn't sleep much last night."

"Donovan! You shouldn't get so worked up over this. It's not that important."

"Yes, it is. It's your shot at hitting the big time and I want you to succeed." He peered at her with an intensity that she couldn't ignore.

Abby was overwhelmed by his generosity. Donovan still had his work on the national campaign, his own hopes and dreams, yet he put everything on hold to cheer her on. He certainly had changed. She wanted to know how much.

"Don, can I ask you something?"

"Shoot," he said, adjusting the blanket over Ari as he brushed a kiss against her cheek.

"Why do you still wear that ring?"

He lifted his hand and studied the amateurish circle of silver on his finger.

"This ring is my touchstone," he said quietly. "It holds a lot of memories for me. It reminds me how far I've come and of how far I need to go."

Abby sniffed. "It's just a hunk of silver, a not very well-made hunk, at that." The crudeness of it embarrassed her. "Why don't you give it to me and I'll rework it into something beautiful."

Donovan shook his head.

"Why not?"

"Because to me it's already beautiful. It was given from a

heart of love," he said, looking her straight in the eye. "Reforming it or pressing out the dents would only erase what I most cherish about it."

"And what's that?" she whispered.

"That a beautiful girl once thought enough of me to trust me with her heart."

Abby gulped. Trusted him? Yes, she'd trusted him totally. And he'd betrayed her.

She never wanted to be that humiliated again.

"Abby? Are you all right?"

"Yes." She smiled at him, squeezed the hand he'd grasped, then drew it away. "We're going to land soon. Shall we wake Ariane?"

Donovan said nothing for several moments, simply watching her with that fierce intensity that made her wiggle uncomfortably.

Fortunately, Ari made the decision herself and sat up, rubbing her eyes.

"Hi, sweetie. We're almost there. Are you okay?" Abby busied herself to avoid Donovan, but when his hand brushed her shoulder as they left their seats, and his arm guided her through the airport, Abby knew she couldn't ignore the way her heart responded to his touch for much longer.

"I'm going to have a gooseneck by the time I get home," Abby complained as she craned her neck to glimpse yet another famous New York sight. "This is amazing."

"It is a unique place in America," Donovan agreed, nodding for her to look at Ari who had her nose glued to the cab window. He'd offered to sit in the middle and let them gawk to their heart's content.

The proximity to Abby was a side benefit he hadn't counted on.

She looked as fresh as a daisy in her navy suit and white silk blouse. Fresh and very lovely. He'd pretended not to hear when the gate attendant, flight crew and cabbie had commented on his lovely family.

From their lips to God's ear. And maybe Abby's, too. Talk about impossible dreams. Abby would be here and he'd be in Denver.

"This is your hotel?" Abby blinked at the elegant structure.

"It's yours, too." Donovan grasped her hand. "You couldn't stay in that other place, Abby. It's too far from the contest and it's not a very safe area." He smiled, hoping she wouldn't be angry. "I asked the office to change it. This way we can all travel together. Saves on cab fare," he added at the last minute.

She studied him a long time before finally nodding.

"Thank you for thinking of me."

If she only knew.

By the time he'd paid the cabbie, their bags were loaded on a trolley. Donovan gripped Ari's hand and followed the bellhop into the hotel. The suite they were shown to, which had a floor-to-ceiling view of Central Park, received exactly the reaction he'd hoped for, which was to make Abby feel special, cherished, valued.

"It's spectacular. Thank you." Abby seemed transfixed by the view.

"You are welcome. Now, what's the schedule for today?"

"The judging was completed this morning. We pick up the entries at one o'clock. There is a welcome reception at seven. The modeling in each category will be done after that, then the winners are announced. You said you'd arranged for someone to model the other pieces?"

Satisfaction surged through him.

"Taken care of. So we've got time to clean up and have lunch. If we're quick."

Donovan set a time limit of twenty minutes for unpacking and Abby was precisely on time.

"I thought I heard someone at the door," she asked, glancing around.

"I sent Ari's dress to be pressed." He ignored Ari's frown. "Ready for lunch?" Donovan suggested they pick up some deli food and eat in the park. "It's a perfect day for it."

They walked along the busy street until Donovan saw the deli his secretary had suggested. With lunch order in hand, they hurried to the park where Ari ate some food, but fed most to the various birds that swooped down. Sometimes she'd forget herself, giggle out loud then slap a hand over her mouth and look to see if they'd noticed anything.

"It's such a frenetic pace outside the park and yet, sitting here, it's like you're in a peaceful little glen." A group of boys on skateboards tore past Abby. "Well, it *was* peaceful."

"How's your coffee?" He chuckled at Abby's grimace. "A little strong?"

"It was nice of you to treat me. But this is about as far from what I'm used to as I can imagine. I far prefer what we have at home."

"No place like home," he agreed, wishing coffee was enough to make her stay in Denver. "Come on, we'd better go get ready to pick up your entries."

For a moment it looked like Ari might mutiny until he reminded her that this was Abby's day and they were here to support her. Ari smiled, nodded and fell into step.

So far, so good.

Now if the rest of his plan went as anticipated, Abby would never forget this evening.

Thank you, God, for sending Donovan.

Abby clung to his arm as they walked into a room teeming with glamorous and well-known people. Picking up her entries was supposed to be a time to schmooze and get to know the judges who couldn't now be swayed but might offer a chance to network and make connections.

"Abby Franklin," she said, over and over, shaking hands as they proceeded down the row.

"This is your husband and daughter?"

"This is Donovan Woodward. I work for Weddings by Woodwards in Denver. Ariane is his daughter."

"Ah." The same response every time was starting to irritate Abby.

"Do I have a smear on my nose? Is my suit dirty?"

"No, to both," Donovan said after dutifully completing a thorough check. "Why?"

Maybe she was imagining the snooty looks. "Let's go look at the exhibits. They'll be displayed for ten more minutes before we can claim them."

Because there was so little time, Abby moved quickly, studying the other contestants' work. Her heart sank at what she saw.

"I should never have entered," she murmured, aghast at the quality of the displays.

"What are you talking about? You won first place for the ring, Abby."

"A fluke. The rest of my stuff doesn't compare to this." Her mother would never let her live this down. Flying to New York, daring to compete with people who had far more knowledge and ability. She could almost hear her mother's words.

"You listen to me, Abby Franklin."

Donovan grasped her hand and drew her and Ari into an alcove. The weight of his palms against her shoulders, the strength of his fingers added a measure of calm. Abby let herself relax into it, allowing the fear and worry to dissipate as he massaged the tension from her neck.

"I'm listening," she whispered.

"We are children of the most high God. He gave you a unique and special talent that no one else here has. He led you into this contest and He will be with you whatever happens, so you get your eyes fixed on Him and forget about everyone else." He chucked her chin. "Do you hear me?"

"Yes, sir." She smiled, but her eyes watered with love for this man who made her feel so cherished and protected. Why couldn't that feeling last forever?

Because Donovan had come home to build his life at Woodwards and her dreams lay here in New York.

But for today he was here, with her, sharing a once-in-a-lifetime opportunity. Abby was going to cherish that.

Thank you, Father. And please help me trust Donovan.

Chapter Fourteen

Donovan had been waiting on tenterhooks for the phone call. Now that he'd received it, he was more nervous than ever.

Ari winced when he pulled her hair too tight.

"Sorry, baby. I'm all thumbs tonight."

With a dour look, she took the sparkly silver barrettes from his hand and walked to a mirror. Using his comb, she arranged her hair perfectly, then turned to grin at him.

"You little minx. You've known how to do it all along."

She smiled, nodded and inclined her head toward Abby's room.

"Yes, I think she'll be very surprised. You won't forget your part, will you? Or get scared or anything? Because you need to tell me now. I don't want Abby to—"

Ariane put two fingers across his lips. When he met her gaze, her long eyelashes dipped down.

"Pray? Yes, of course." He did, asking God for help and wisdom. He'd planned everything, hoping Abby would win. If she didn't, he was going to need some holy guidance to help her.

"Donovan?" Abby's fingertips tapped against his door. "We should leave soon."

"We're ready." He opened the door and nearly choked. "Wow, you look good."

"Thank you."

Abby wore the red dress she'd worn for his grandmother's party, only this time she'd paired it with golden helix earrings that dangled specifically to emphasize her slim neck. She'd wrapped a wide belt of the same twisting style around her narrow waist.

"Can you walk in those shoes?" he asked, staring at the coils of gold circling around her feet.

"Let's see." She walked carefully across the room.

That's when he noticed she wore his bracelet on her left wrist.

"I think this occasion merits it," she murmured, catching his stare. Then she saw Ari. "Oh, honey, you look like a fairy princess."

Ari beamed. That, of course, had been her goal.

"And you, Donovan, you look very good, too," Abby said simply, her eyes sparkling. "I'd forgotten how well you wear a tux."

"Kind of reminds you of that grad night, doesn't it?" Donovan gulped. Why had he said that?

"Yes." Abby grinned at him and his breath returned. "Shall we go?"

Once again, the welcome reception was teeming with notables and those nobody knew. Donovan was glad they had a few moments of privacy.

"Abby, I wanted to tell you some—"

Someone interrupted, and then another until Donovan could only stand back and wait his turn. In that moment he realized how much he enjoyed *not* being the center of attention. In the old days he'd probably have made some silly remark to deflect attention from Abby onto himself, but tonight Abby's success filled his heart.

He and Ari sat and watched and smiled until she finally returned.

"Mercy." Abby fanned her cheeks. "I'm hot."

"You look perfectly at home here. Like one of the big shots." He touched her cheek. "You're flushed. Would you like something to drink?"

"No. I think we're supposed to get ready for the show now. Can you come?"

"Of course," he said as if he'd actually considered doing anything else. In the wings he saw Art and left long enough to slip him a small box. "Everything okay?"

"Perfect." They shared a glance of mutual understanding, then Donovan hurried back to Abby.

"What's Art doing here?" Abby demanded, suspicion glinting in her eyes.

"He wants to give Grandmother her ring tonight. I told him he wouldn't have to wait much longer."

"Oh." Abby frowned. "I have to get in the line. Will you be okay?"

"Yes." He leaned forward and kissed her hard on the lips. "Trust, Abby. Just a little longer."

"What do you—" The stage boss hurried her away and she could ask no more.

Donovan followed Ari to where the models of Abby's jewelry waited behind the stage curtain.

"Do not lose this child," he warned them, then kissed Ari's head. "This is for Abby, remember, Ari?"

She grinned at him, nodded then pointed. The first entry was on stage.

Donovan was on pins and needles until they called Abby's name. She was supposed to give a brief explanation of each piece, but as Winifred and Art walked on stage, Abby could only stare. But that was okay because God had given Donovan Woodward the gift of the gab and for once he was going to use it for someone else.

He walked up beside Abby, slid his arm around her waist and leaned toward the microphone.

"A diamond ring," he said as photos of Winifred's ring hit the large screen televisions around the room. A gasp went up from the crowd. "Is it an heirloom? Or did our happy couple only make their pledges to each other tonight?"

When he'd finished that dialogue, Olivia emerged, her neckline draped in Abby's delightful anniversary necklace, her hand wrapped in Reese's. Then Sara followed with Cade. They walked hand-in-hand across the stage, Sara's pregnancy emphasized. Her white gown was covered by a shawl on which two multistoned butterflies perched, mother and child.

"Perfect for those enchanting moments a couple wants to cherish for the rest of their lives, a moment that builds their heritage."

Then Emily, Reese's adopted daughter, dressed in a pop/hip style, pranced onto the stage to rock music, showing off her graduation watch.

"Graduation, a perfect time to commemorate the strides taken and vistas yet to find. Steps commemorated in a way your young adult will never forget."

The crowd went wild. Donovan had to wait for silence. Abby stood on her tiptoes.

"You planned all this?" she asked, her face stunned. "For me?"

"Who else? Can't talk now. Job's not done."

She glanced to the side and caught her breath as Ariane stepped forward hesitantly, then backed up. Donovan held his breath and prayed. Finally, with Katie's help, Ari half pushed, half dragged Brett and Brady, Reese's twins, onto the stage. The cute suits Donovan had requested were in a bad state, shirttails hanging, bow ties askew, pant legs half-stuck in socks. Once they spotted their father, the boys straightened, hung on to Ari's hands and walked with her.

The crowd was enchanted.

"Ah, those years, when you never know what might happen."

As if to emphasize that, Brady tripped and landed on his butt.

Reese rescued him before he could bawl. In doing so he showed off the silver band around the boy's wrist.

"We all hear about it. Child abductions are on the rise. How wonderful to know modern technology to track your child can be hidden inside a bracelet that looks like a play watch. And styled to be as individual as your heritage."

Right on cue, Ari held out her arm. Brett glared at her and when she tried to show his watch, he jerked away. Reese cleared his throat. Brett looked at him, bent over to tie his shoe and let everyone see his arm, grinning wickedly into the camera.

The crowd hooted.

"The Heritage Collection." Donovan paused to be certain they'd catch the name. "By Abigail Franklin."

He stepped back and eased Abby forward to receive the praise she so rightly deserved. Inside, he gave thanks for the love of a wonderful family.

Then they moved en masse to the side of the stage to wait for the judges' announcement. Abby's fingers laced through his and she pressed a kiss against his cheek.

"Thank you, Don. Thank you so much."

Five years ago he'd made the right decision to propose to her. This was the woman he wanted to marry. It had nothing to do with winning; it had to do with his heritage, one he wanted to build with her.

"I love you, Abby."

She blinked, tried to smile, but tears welled in her eyes. Donovan wanted to explain, but there was no time as the master of ceremonies began speaking.

"We had over five hundred entries in this contest. There were the ordinary, the extraordinary and the utterly incredible. Wonderful work by talented designers who know their market and strive to reach it. Tonight we announce Abigail Franklin as our contest winner."

Incredibly, Abby looked shocked, almost frightened by the

announcement. Donovan pressed a hand against her back and urged her forward to receive her reward.

"Miss Franklin, will you tell us how the Heritage concept came to you?"

"From a family home called Heritage House." Abby's shaky voice firmed with every word. "Each room seemed to me to carry a reminder of times in a family's life when pivotal events added another layer to their lives, moments that should be honored, cherished." She turned, held out a hand to indicate her models. "Behind me is a family who esteems such multigenerational moments and takes special care to celebrate each one. I must thank the wonderful, unpredictable Woodward family of Denver. They embody the essence of my Heritage line."

The applause grew loud and people surged forward as Abby received her award. Donovan wanted to stay with her, but he had to care for Ariane.

"Art and I are getting married, Donovan." His pink-cheeked grandmother held out her ring for him to see. "He had Abby make it, especially for me."

"Yes, I know." He hugged her close. What a special woman. "You don't mind?"

"I'm ecstatic. Although I should warn Art about your temper."

"Stop teasing her, bro." Reese thumped him on the back. "Good job out there. Maybe we should conscript you to announce at Grandmother's next showing."

"Don't think I wouldn't ace it, too." Donovan thanked his family for their help. "Abby had no idea, but I think she appreciated your performances."

"Abby adored your performances. All of them. I'll never be able to thank you enough." Abby hugged each Woodward. "I owe you."

"Nonsense. You're one of us and we stick together." Winifred snuck another look at her ring.

"Mrs. Woodward, the entire 'Heritage' collection is yours.

Donovan and I were talking about Woodwards' need to draw from a multigenerational pot and that inspired me. Then you asked me to use those old pieces of yours, so you made it all happen. It's only fair that what the gems are now become part of Donovan's new 'Generations' campaign." She handed over the velvet box which held all the pieces except Winifred's ring.

Winifred opened her mouth once, closed it and opened it again. When she finally found her voice, it was unsteady, brimming with tears.

"It's a wonderful gift, Abby. Thank you. In return, I insist on paying you for all you've spent on these marvelous things, especially your time."

Donovan's soul wanted to yell for joy when Abby shook her head.

"I've already been rewarded," she murmured, "so many times. May I congratulate you and Art officially?"

Donovan waited impatiently while his family, other contestants, judges and several famous New York jewelers congratulated Abby. He wanted to get her alone, to find out if she'd understood his hurried profession of love, but Abby seemed happy to prolong each moment and he couldn't begrudge her that.

Because most of the family was returning to Denver tonight, they soon departed. Gradually the crowds melted until only one man remained. Donovan saw him give Abby a business card which she tucked into her evening bag. She nodded and he left.

"Ready to head back to the hotel?" he asked, holding Ari who'd fallen asleep on his shoulder and wishing she'd explain who the man was.

"Yes, please. It was a wonderful night, Don. Thank you for arranging all that. They went to so much trouble for me. Even this little one is worn out." She touched Ari's tiny fingers.

"We wanted to do it. You've worked so hard on this project, how could we not be here for you?"

They climbed into a cab. Abby said nothing, but her eyes told him something was wrong.

"What is it?"

"I only wish my parents—" She broke off, shook her head. "Never mind."

"We asked them," Donovan told her, unwilling to hide Mary's refusal to attend. "Grandmother even had plane tickets. They wouldn't come."

"Probably thought I'd lose," Abby joked, the sheen of tears glossing her eyes. She tossed her head back, forcing a smile. "Don't mind me. I think I must be tired. Everything seems so unreal. Winning that contest, having your family here as models—" She shook her head. "Unbelievable."

"Totally believable," he countered. "You've reached your goal, Abby. What's next?"

Abby studied him for a long time before she whispered, "I don't know."

"About what I said," he began, but the cabdriver was speedier than he'd expected. They were back at the hotel and the opportunity was lost.

"Ariane looked so pretty, walking onto the stage with the twins."

"Yeah." Donovan grinned, as proud as any father. "She even tried to get those two wild things into line. My little Ari is changing."

They rode the elevator in an uneasy silence.

Donovan unlocked the door, led the way inside the suite. Someone had already been in to switch on the lights.

"Do you need help to get her to bed?"

He'd been going to refuse, but Donovan changed his mind and nodded.

"That would be great."

They worked together to remove Ariane's pretty dress and replace it with her pink pajamas. But there were only so many jobs and they were completed too fast. Donovan tucked the covers around the tiny body. Abby bent to hug her. As she rose Ari's eyelids fluttered.

Donovan bent and whispered, "We're back in your lovely room at the hotel in New York. It's very late, sweetheart. Go back to sleep."

He leaned over to hug her and felt her tiny arms wind around his neck.

"I love you, Ari," he said, as he did every night.

"I love you, too, Daddy Donovan."

He opened his mouth to say more, but there was no point. Ariane turned her cheek against the pillow as her lashes flickered downward and she drifted off.

"Did you hear that?" He twisted his head to find Abby who stood silently weeping. "She spoke. Out loud."

"I know."

Donovan burst to his feet, unable to contain the joy that filled him. He drew Abby out of the room and closed the door almost shut.

"She spoke, Abby. She really spoke." He pulled her into his arms, swinging her round and round as he laughed, his heart so full of joy that he could no longer find words to express it. It was Abby's face that made him stop.

No longer smiling. Big, hazel eyes glinting gold sparks at him.

He let her go, stepped back. "You're mad at me."

"Why did you do it again? I was almost ready to trust you, to believe you actually felt something for me. And you had to ruin that."

"Huh?" Donovan scanned the past four hours in his mind about what he'd done and came up blank.

"I worked hard for this night. I spent hours working on those designs."

"And you won. I thought I was helping you celebrate."

"Really? That's why you couldn't let me enjoy it, why you

had to say those words again and bring back the past." She advanced on him, her nostrils flaring. "What did you think, Don? That I'd swoon in your arms, play along, let myself be fooled again?"

Ah, she thought he'd only said it as a game, he realized.

"Is it so hard for you to be out of the limelight for an hour or two, to let someone else be in it?"

"No," he said sincerely, sitting down on the sofa and opening one of the frosty cans of soda. "No, it's not hard for me at all. I sat there tonight, watching everyone applaud for you, and I thought how much I'd like to do that for the rest of my life."

"What?" Anger still sparked in those golden depths.

"I figured something out, Abby, something I never even imagined five years ago." He paused. "I don't have to be 'on' all the time. Not anymore. I finally figured out that I don't need to hide the real me because God already knows who that is and he's okay with it. And so am I."

"Then why say that you loved me?"

"Because I meant it. I love you. I always have. My dense brain just took its own sweet time to process that information. And I allowed a certain person to fool me, but we can talk about that later." Donovan stayed where he was, refusing to push or cajole Abby. "I have never been more proud of you, Abby. To know you, to watch you fight through deep disappointment and shattered hope and still keep digging for answers to your questions—" He shook his head. "That took guts. It also made me realize that as Ari grows up, I want her to see that modeled. She already wants to be you, Abby."

Abby groped her way to the sofa opposite his and sat down as if her legs could no longer hold her up.

"I'm not playing games, Abby. I'm not going to change my mind in a week or two. I'm not leaving Denver and I'm not running away. Not ever again." He smiled as the certainty of those statements echoed in his heart. "I loved you five years ago, but it was a new love, easily attacked. I love you now the way I believe God expects a man to love a woman. I want to cherish you, adore you and always, always put you first."

Still Abby said nothing.

Donovan was beginning to worry. For the first time in his life he'd laid himself and his hopes and dreams totally on the line and there was no return, no way to take it back or pretend he'd been joking.

Now it was all up to Abby.

Chapter Fifteen

Abby's dream had come true. She had achieved her design goal.

But her heart wasn't happy.

Because Donovan was what it craved. He made her world light up no matter what the weather. He pushed her, encouraged her and even propped her up, when necessary. But he also let her down.

You have to trust.

That was the key, wasn't it? Bad things happened. Changes occurred. Nothing was secure.

The only way to make it through was to trust.

"I love you, too," she whispered, praying for wisdom.

"You had to wait so long to say it," he complained, but a moment later he had her in his arms and conversation was impossible.

Abby kissed him back, needing the reassurance of holding him because everything about this evening was unbelievable.

"When can we get married?" His hand traced a line from the end of her eyebrow to the corner of her mouth where he planted a kiss. "Next month?"

"Donovan! What's the rush?"

"Rush?" He pulled back, indignation spewing out. "It's been five years!"

They argued back and forth good-naturedly until the wee hours of the morning when Abby lost track of his comments because of her yawns.

"I do truly love you, Donovan, but I have to get some sleep. Today has been exhausting."

"You don't know the half of it," he complained, but he allowed her to leave his embrace. "No goodnight kiss?"

"You've had it. Besides if we start that again—" She shook her head at him. "Goodnight, my darling Donovan."

She fluttered her fingers and escaped to her room where beautiful dreams ended far too quickly because of a dark-headed sprite who bounced on her bed.

"Good morning, Abby."

"Good morning, Ariane. How are you?"

"Fine." She flopped on the side of the bed and swung her feet. "Donovan says if you don't get up soon we're going to miss our flight."

"It can't be that late." Abby glanced at the clock and jumped out of bed. She paused a moment to crouch beside Ariane. "I'm very glad you've decided to speak, sweetie. I like to have my friends talk to me. Can you tell me why you couldn't talk before?"

Ari met her question with a very serious look.

"I think I had to be sure," she whispered.

"Sure of what?" But in that moment Abby knew. "That you could trust us?"

Ari nodded.

"But you know now, don't you? You know you can trust Donovan and me with anything and we'll be there for you." Again Ari nodded, a huge smile spread across her face. "Good." Abby hugged her again, so grateful for the little girl's voice. "When you speak, it's like music to me. I can't hear enough."

"Then I'll never be quiet," Ariane teased.

"Well, you'll have to talk to Donovan while I shower. Tell him I'll be out in ten, maybe fifteen minutes."

It turned out to be more than twenty, but Donovan didn't seem to mind.

"Good morning," he murmured before he kissed her.

"Hi," she said shyly, noticing, from the corner of her eye, Ariane's intense study of them. "Donovan." She whispered for him to stop.

"I've explained to Ariane that you and I love each other and are going to get married."

"Does that mean you'll move into our house, Abby?" Ariane asked.

"Would you like that?" How did one go about this step-mother business?

"Yes." When there was a knock on the suite's door, Ariane raced to answer it and explained to room service exactly how she wanted the tray placed. "This is a special breakfast," she said.

"Every one you don't miss is, child." The elderly man chuckled and pocketed Donovan's tip. "Thank you, sir. Miss, ma'am. Have a great day."

They shared a wonderful meal, laughing, giggling and every so often, talking about the future. But it was soon time to leave. Abby wanted to talk to Donovan on the flight back, but she was so tired and Ariane was so wide awake. Abby fell asleep a few moments after takeoff and never woke up until they hit the ground in Denver.

"Well, that was rude of me," she said.

"You needed the rest." Donovan pretended to help her and sneaked a kiss. "Ready?"

"Yes."

To Abby's surprise, they ended up at Weddings by Woodwards. The entire staff applauded when she entered. She was amazed by their generous goodwill and by Winifred's insistence that the store be closed while they celebrated. Even her parents arrived and congratulated her. Mary mumbled something about a flash in the pan while her father simply smiled. Abby refused to let her mother's lapse ruin her joy.

"You look happy," Sara murmured as they sat together after enjoying a feast and a lot of teasing jokes.

"I am. Do you mind if I love your brother?"

"Would it make a difference?"

"No. I can't help it, I do." Abby laughed with her, sharing the joy of love.

"I know exactly how you feel."

"Abby, there's a call for you. From New York. Shall I ask them to call back tomorrow?" Katie offered.

"No, it's fine. I probably forgot something at the hotel." She walked to reception and picked up the phone, glad for the silence. "Hello?"

"Is this Abby Franklin?"

"Yes. Who is calling?"

"Jonathan Reed. Do you know who I am?"

"Of course, Mr. Reed. How can I help you?"

"We would like to offer you the position of head designer in our jewelry department." The CEO of New York's most famous jeweler named a salary that made Abby's eyes bug.

"But I already have a job, with Weddings by Woodwards."

"Surely now that you've achieved this new success, you'll want to move on, reach for a new level of achievement?"

"Of course, but—"

"I'm sure you need time to consider our offer, but we in turn must fill the position as quickly as possible. Will three days allow you enough time to decide?"

Three days to decide her future? Abby inhaled.

"I will give you my decision about your job offer in three days, Mr. Reed."

"Great. Here's my number. I look forward to hearing from you."

Abby stood holding the receiver long after he'd hung up. The offer was incredible, unbelievable. But what about Donovan? What about the future they'd only begun to discuss? What about Weddings by Woodwards?

"Abby?" Donovan stood in the doorway. "Anything wrong?"

"No." She opened her mouth to explain, but closed it again when Fiona insisted she come see the cake they'd made.

The rest of the day passed in a blur. By the time Donovan took her home, Abby was no longer sure which way her world spun.

"Thank you for the lovely party," she said, touching his arm.

"You're welcome."

He seemed cooler, withdrawn.

"Are you okay?" she murmured.

"Sure. Why not? Donovan Woodward doesn't get tired." He slanted a smile at her, but it lacked his usual verve. He pulled up to her place and turned to face her. "I should tell you that I won't be around tomorrow. I've got some appointments until late in the evening."

"Oh." She pouted for a moment. "I could make dinner for you and Ari."

"She's staying overnight with Jessica."

"Oh." Wasn't he even going to kiss her goodnight? "Donovan, what did you mean when you said someone fooled you?"

He paused for a long time, studying her. Then he smiled.

"Not tonight, okay?"

"Okay." She felt abandoned, as if he'd dumped her again. "Well, I'd better go in. Bye."

"Abby?"

"Yes?" She turned from opening her door and felt his lips press against hers in a hard, almost desperate kiss.

"I love you very much," he whispered, peering into her eyes as if to imprint his words.

"Good thing," she teased, grazing her fingers against his cheek. "Because I love you, too. Goodnight."

"Yeah."

He waited until she had the house door open, then roared away.

Abby watched for a minute, frowning. Then she shrugged and walked inside.

Tomorrow she'd find out what was wrong. Tonight she was going to savor the thrill of having received a wonderful job offer.

"Thank you, Lord," she whispered, peering into the night sky. "Thank you for all of it."

"You're sure, Ari? You didn't mistake a word or anything."

"No. I told you what she said. I didn't make a mistake." Her dark eyes swirled with questions. "Is Abby going away?"

"I don't know yet, sweetheart, but let's not tell anyone what you overheard. Abby will tell us when she's ready."

So Abby had received a job offer from New York. Why was he surprised after the accolades she'd received?

"Are you ready for school?"

Ariane nodded.

"Then let's go." Donovan dropped Ari off before heading for Woodwards.

He did have a meeting today, one, with his grandmother. She was full of chitchat, delighted about her engagement and Abby's great achievements.

"She was offered a job," he said when she gave him an opportunity to speak.

"From Reeds?"

"You expected it?"

"Of course. Abby is talented. Lots of companies are going to try to win her."

"And you won't mind losing her?"

Winifred sniffed.

"Of course I'll mind losing her. But I want the best for Abby and if going to New York is what she wants, then I support her all the way."

"That's very gracious of you."

"Gracious? Pfui!" Winifred stood in front of him. "Loving someone means you want the best for them, no matter how it affects you. Remember faith, hope and love. The greatest of these is love, but it doesn't work without faith and hope to back it up."

"Yeah."

"Do you love Abby, Donovan?"

"Yes."

"How much?" Winifred patted his cheek before picking up the phone and giving directions for her day.

Donovan left the building, reminded of the time she'd told him he'd know the right time to prove his love. In a nearby park he found a lush green spot in the sunshine where he could talk to God about his next step, one that God's man, a man of integrity would take to make sure he didn't lose the girl of his heart.

"It's a great offer, Mom, and I think I might take it."

"But you can't!" Her mother collapsed onto a dining room chair as tears welled.

"It's not that I *want* to go, Mom. Woodwards has been like my second family. They've done so much for me." Even thinking of it made her hesitate, however Abby pushed on. "But if I don't take this opportunity, I'll never know how much I could have achieved."

"Your achievements mean more to you than us?" Her mother continued to weep. "I've prayed and prayed for this not to happen."

"What? Why? Why can you never support me, Mom?"

"I support you. Of course I do. But New York?" She sniffed, dabbed at her tears. "We'll never see you."

Abby opened her mouth to reassure and caught sight of her father's eyes. Fear lay crouched there. Fear and desperation. And suddenly she understood. It wasn't about her career. It was about being left alone, abandoned to fight the world without her there to help. It was about losing their only child.

Am I making a mistake, God? Is this not from you?

Abby patted her mother's shoulder.

"Nothing has been decided. I haven't even told anyone else because I wanted to think about it a little longer. I'm not abandoning you, Mom and Dad. I'll always be here if you need me."

"We'll always need our Abby," her father said.

"I'll always need you, too," she said, watching her mother turn away. "Now are you going to sample some of this ice-cream cake, Dad, or let it melt?"

He dug in eagerly and Abby took the opportunity to corner her mother in the kitchen.

"Donovan mentioned something about someone fooling him five years ago. He seems to be under the impression that I won some kind of scholarship to a college near New York." She didn't have to go on, she saw the guilt rush across her mother's face. "You made him go away, didn't you, Mother? You deliberately ruined my happiness."

Anger built into a tsunami that Abby could scarcely hold back. She wanted to rant and rage at her mother until she saw the way her face crumpled and heard her beg forgiveness.

"I know it was wrong. May God forgive me, I knew that if you found out you'd never forgive me, but I couldn't stop myself. I couldn't bear for you to leave us. The Woodwards have several children, we had only one." She sniffed, rubbed her eyes. "I know now that you'll probably hate me, especially because you've fallen for him again."

"I never really stopped loving Donovan," Abby said. She sank down onto a chair, thinking over the many times Donovan had hinted at the truth. "What did you tell him?"

"That you only pretended to love him because you were so insecure. That you disliked children, that your whole world revolved around getting into that college and moving to New York," she admitted shame-faced. "That you never felt anything for him but friendship and you didn't know how to let him down easily. That you would marry him because you felt you had to, not because you loved him."

She would have gone on, but Abby couldn't listen to any more. It was all too sad.

"I'm so sorry, Abby. Will you forgive me?" Mary said.

What was the point of making her mother suffer more? Abby couldn't find it in her heart. God had given her a second chance at love. She wasn't going to waste it.

"You'll have to ask Donovan's forgiveness."

"I will, I promise. I'm glad you've found each other again. Truly. Since I've been doing this Bible study the guilt has been overwhelming."

They talked for a long time after that. By the time Abby returned to work, the slate between her mother and her was clean. But in the back of her mind, the sad looks her parents had tried to hide would not be erased. They felt they were losing their daughter.

The afternoon passed slowly as Abby completed her tasks. Each interaction seemed somehow more poignant, more meaningful. Would she have this same one-on-one rapport in New York?

"Abby?"

She glanced up from her sketch and saw Ari waiting in the doorway.

"Hi, honey. I didn't know you were coming here today."

"I got Mrs. Beasley to bring me. I need to talk to you."

"Okay. Should we go out in the courtyard?" This had to be important. Abby rose and prepared to leave.

"No. Here is fine." Ari sat down. "Can I ask you a question?"

"Sure, sweetie. Go ahead."

"Well, Donovan and I were talking about my dad last night and I got thinking. If Donovan couldn't be there, would you? If I needed you, I mean. Granny Winnie always talks about putting love first and I thought maybe when you guys get married, you wouldn't need me, but I'd still need you. So I thought I'd like to know—do you love me, Abby?"

"Oh, honey." Abby rose, walked around the desk and knelt beside the girl. She touched her hair, her cheek, and wrapped her fingers around her soft hand. "Don't you know that if you weren't here," she tapped her chest, "my heart would be missing a big chunk? You make me laugh. And when you wouldn't talk, you made me cry because I love you so much and I want you to be happy. I love you very much, Ariane. Even though I love Donovan, that doesn't mean there isn't enough room for you, too."

"Oh."

"Love is kind of like a sponge. It just keeps soaking up more and more people." Ariane didn't look completely satisfied, so Abby continued. "Whenever you need me, I'll always be there for you, darling. You just let me know. You're stuck in my heart and you're not getting out."

Ariane hugged her.

"Thanks, Abby."

"You're welcome. Now you scoot home because I don't think you're supposed to be here, are you? Donovan's out today."

"He's sitting in the park. He said he needs time to think." Ariane jumped off her chair. "But I hafta go now. I need to tell Jessica. Bye, Abby." She raced out of the room and down the hall, calling for Mrs. Beasley.

Donovan was in the park thinking? About what?

A fist closed around Abby's heart and squeezed so tight she could hardly breathe. Surely he wouldn't run away again. Not after all they'd said to each other.

But on the heels of that thought came Ariane's words, her obvious yearning to be reassured. Moving to New York would mean losing precious moments like those. There was no guarantee Donovan would want to move, especially after barely settling into Heritage House.

Memories of that house made Abby pause and consider

what she might potentially be giving up. Was attaining her goal of New York worth the sacrifices she'd have to make? Would it fill the hole of losing Donovan?

Verses from the Bible study she'd completed filled Abby's mind. God's love was unconditional; it would be there whether she achieved her goals or not.

Abby always assumed she could never be good enough. But now she realized how wrong her thinking had been. Technically, she could never be good enough to earn God's love. But God loved her anyway. Depending on God and letting him lead her was the only way to fill that void in her heart. Donovan couldn't, neither could Ariane. They were human, they made mistakes. But God would always be there, loving her.

"I'm an idiot," she whispered, squeezing her eyes shut tight. "You gave me a man who loves me, a little girl who needs me and two families to support all three of us. Help me be worthy of your gifts."

Then she picked up the phone. "Mr. Reed, I'm so sorry but I must decline your very generous offer." They exchanged pleasantries and then Abby hung up, knowing in her heart that she'd made the right decision.

Now she wanted to tell Donovan.

"Katie, I'm going to be out for the rest of the day."

Abby drove with her radio on, singing along to Point of Grace's cheery song about faith. The last note strangled in her throat as she turned onto Donovan's street. A giant For Sale sign sat beneath the spruce bows.

He was moving. She'd finally trusted him and now he was running away again. All those promises—why?

Pain like she'd never known shafted through Abby. She flicked on her signal light to drive away. But an inner voice prompted her to think it through. God was with her. He'd directed her decisions. Wasn't it better to face the truth with him in her corner than to wait five more years?

The drive up to the house took almost two minutes. Donovan was standing on the front step, talking to the real estate agent. When he saw her, he strode forward. Abby jumped out of the car, anger dogging her.

"You're leaving? Selling this perfect house and running? Why? Because you don't want to marry me?" She shook off his restraining hand. "You only had to say so, Donovan. What about Ari? This is her home now. You can't expect her to give up Jessica and Mrs. Beasley and—"

To her utter disgrace, Abby burst into tears.

"Oh, Abby." Donovan pulled her into his arms and held her until she stopped struggling. "Let me explain."

"It's not me you have to explain to," she sniffed.

"Yes, it is. You're the woman I love and I should have told you first only I just decided and—"

"Never mind. It doesn't really matter, does it, Donovan? We've been through all this before. Goodbye." She turned and walked to her car. Somehow God would help her get over him. Somehow she'd learn to move on.

"Abby, I'm selling the house so I can move to New York with you. As soon as we get married."

She liked the sound of the married part. Wait a minute.

"New York?" Abby whirled around to stare at him. "I'm not going to New York."

"But—your job?" Donovan frowned, glanced behind him to Ari who stood in the doorway watching. "I thought—" His forehead pleated in that endearing way that made her stomach tilt. "You're not moving?"

"Nope. You're not running away?" she asked.

"From you? Not a chance, babe."

"Oh."

Someone cleared her throat.

"I'm guessing Heritage House will not be back on the market anytime soon?" the real estate agent said.

"No way," Abby said. "I found this place and I intend to live here. With my husband and our daughter."

"Okay then." The real estate agent smiled, climbed in her car and drove away.

"I'll go to New York if you want, Abby. Anywhere, anytime," Donovan murmured, holding her stare with his own. "I know what I want now."

"What's that?" Those amazing blue eyes had always made her weak in the knees.

"You. I want to share my life, all of my life with you, Abby. I want you to know exactly who I am, secrets and all. I want us to live with God at the center of our lives. I want us to raise Ari to know that she is a child of God."

"Is that all?"

Donovan shook his head, kept walking nearer until he was three inches away.

"I want to love you, Abby Franklin. I want you to be so confident in my love for you that you'll never doubt me or it again."

"I want that, too."

Donovan's unblinking stare finally ended when he looked down, working the battered old silver ring free of his finger. He went down on one knee in front of her and held out the ring.

"Abby, darling Abby, will you please marry me?"

She studied the ring with a wrinkled nose.

"On one condition."

"Which is?"

"I get to design our rings."

Donovan rose, slid the silver ring back onto his pinkie finger.

"Not this one," he said as he drew her into his arms. "It's part of our heritage."

"I'm good with that," she said right before they sealed their troth with a kiss.

Epilogue

"**W**eddings by Woodwards has always prided itself on perfectly managed nuptials that reflects the bride and groom's tastes. In this case, I think we've managed admirably. Don't you, darling?"

Art panned the interior of Heritage House. His attention strayed outside where Mark and Mary, Fiona and Thomas and Abby and Donovan swayed happily together under moonlight and a few twinkling candles.

"Perfectly. As usual."

"Thank you, dear."

"Now when will it be our turn? Or is Katie your next project?"

"No." Winifred stared at the stars. "I think God has something different planned for her."

"Granny Winnie?"

"Yes, my darling Ari."

"Brett and Brady are ruining the wedding cake."

Winifred smiled. "It's only plastic under the icing, dear. I have the real one safely stored away."

"I've got to tell Jessica." She raced away, her princess dress billowing out behind her.

"I've been very blessed, Art." Winifred pointed to Donovan and Abby who were sneaking away from the crowd. "God has been good to my family. I'd like to celebrate by dancing."

"Took you long enough." He led her onto the floor.

"By the way, next Friday might be a good day for our wedding."

Art's embrace conveyed his agreement.

Abby leaned against Donovan's broad chest and took one last look at their reception.

"It really is Heritage House, isn't it?"

"Mmm." Donovan slid something around her neck. "You gave me my fantastic ring. This is my wedding gift to you. It's old-fashioned maybe, but it's at least a piece of jewelry I can give you that you haven't designed."

Abby leaned forward and stared into the mirror across the hall.

"Pearls! They're gorgeous. Thank you, darling."

"They remind me of you. Perfectly formed, polished, glowing and enduring."

"Because of God." She looped her arms around his neck.

"They're also my promise to you never to run away again, no matter what your mother says."

"I'm not worried. I'm finally at peace, Don. The past is healed, I don't have to gain approval. The future is waiting for me. Somehow I'll find a new relationship with my mom and build a stronger one with Ari. With your help."

He cupped her face in his hands and sweetly kissed her.

"I'm available anytime you need me. Mrs. Woodward."

"I'm glad you said that, Mr. Woodward, because my newest goal is for you to get us out of here so we can be alone together."

"That's a goal I can help you with and a promise I'm prepared to keep."

They sneaked away from the crowd and quietly drove to a secret place to begin building their own heritage, with God as the foundation.

* * * * *

Dear Reader,

I'm so glad you dropped by for another visit at Weddings by Woodwards. How the family has grown and changed. Her prodigal grandson's return allowed Winifred to see the changes God had wrought in him and gave her great satisfaction when Donovan finally realized his best love was his first love. In Abby, Winifred saw potential and nurtured it to a great result. Best of all, Winifred found her own special love.

I hope you've enjoyed all three of my stories about this amazing family who triumph through pain and loss. As always, I'd love to hear from you. Feel free to contact me at loisricher@yahoo.com, or by snail mail at Box 639, Nipawin, SK, Canada S0E 1E0. To see upcoming titles, go to www.loisricher.com.

Until next time, I pray you find a place with the Father where peace abides, where hope prevails and where love lasts forever.

Blessings,

Lois
Richer

QUESTIONS FOR DISCUSSION

1. Both Abby and Donovan had goals they were determined to achieve. Is goal setting important? Suggest ways we can focus our efforts in life through goals.

2. Pose situations both from the story and from life when a goal can become an impediment to following God.

3. When Donovan's friend died and he was left to care for his goddaughter, he experienced a new awareness of the importance of how he lived his life. Compare your own experiences when life has thrown a curveball that had awakened you to what you were missing.

4. Abby's mother refused to accept her choices. Discuss the ways she manipulates her daughter and relate this to real-life situations where parents can't or won't accept their children as they are and the damage this can cause.

5. Suggest times when it's necessary to redirect a child's focus and times when it is important to let the child experience the results of his/her own choices. Consider when a parent's wishes become detrimental to his/her child.

6. Donovan was well aware of his shortcomings and feared reverting to his old habit of running away from problems, but found Abby's support a great help. Discuss ways we can overcome our own failures by having someone who feels free to check up on us when necessary.

7. Consider the ways Heritage House impacted both Donovan and Abby and led them both to the realization that each still had feelings for the other.

8. Ariane's refusal to speak after her father's death forced Donovan to dig deeper to communicate with her on a more intimate level. Discuss how we allow barriers to keep us from speaking what is in our hearts.

9. Abby felt jealous of the Woodwards' ability to reach out to God and have their prayers answered. Offer experiences in which you've envied another Christian and how you overcame that envy.

10. Although she wanted to be close to God, Abby felt disappointed that He never seemed to answer her. Talk about times you've felt disappointed in God's response to your needs. Suggest ways to understand His silence.

11. Weddings by Woodwards was a family-run enterprise. Propose situations in which working for/with your family could be problematic and ways to resolve conflicts.

12. To cover her bruised ego and hurting heart, Abby pretended that Donovan's five-year absence didn't hurt and she concentrated on her work. Offer suggestions as to when work is a panacea and when it can begin to interfere with living.

13. In New York, Abby found success. She reached her goal. Discuss achievements and how they can help us discover more about ourselves and our relationship with God.

14. Abby's ultimate goal, to become a designer of note and prestige, culminated in a job offer which she ultimately declined. Do you think she should have accepted? Talk about how we make choices and how they affect us.

15. Ultimately, Donovan and Abby both achieve their goals. Discuss how their goals altered and what they learned from achieving them and apply that to your own situation to determine if it's time to reassess your own goals and the purpose for them.

REQUEST YOUR FREE BOOKS!

2 FREE INSPIRATIONAL NOVELS
PLUS 2
FREE
MYSTERY GIFTS

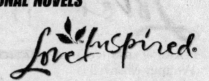

YES! Please send me 2 FREE Love Inspired® novels and my 2 FREE mystery gifts (gifts are worth about $10). After receiving them, if I don't wish to receive any more books, I can return the shipping statement marked "cancel". If I don't cancel, I will receive 4 brand-new novels every month and be billed just $4.24 per book in the U.S. or $4.74 per book in Canada. That's a savings of over 20% off the cover price. It's quite a bargain! Shipping and handling is just 50¢ per book.* I understand that accepting the 2 free books and gifts places me under no obligation to buy anything. I can always return a shipment and cancel at any time. Even if I never buy another book, the two free books and gifts are mine to keep forever.

113 IDN EYK2   313 IDN EYLE

Name	(PLEASE PRINT)	
Address		Apt. #
City	State/Prov.	Zip/Postal Code

Signature (if under 18, a parent or guardian must sign)

Mail to Steeple Hill Reader Service:
IN U.S.A.: P.O. Box 1867, Buffalo, NY 14240-1867
IN CANADA: P.O. Box 609, Fort Erie, Ontario L2A 5X3

Not valid to current subscribers of Love Inspired books.

Want to try two free books from another series?
Call 1-800-873-8635 or visit www.morefreebooks.com

* Terms and prices subject to change without notice. Prices do not include applicable taxes. Sales tax applicable in N.Y. Canadian residents will be charged applicable provincial taxes and GST. Offer not valid in Quebec. This offer is limited to one order per household. All orders subject to approval. Credit or debit balances in a customer's account(s) may be offset by any other outstanding balance owed by or to the customer. Please allow 4 to 6 weeks for delivery. Offer available while quantities last.

LIREG09

HEARTWARMING INSPIRATIONAL ROMANCE

Experience stories
centered on love and faith
with a variety of romances
just for you,
with 10 books every month!

Love Inspired®:
Enjoy four contemporary,
heartwarming romances every month.

Love Inspired® Historical:
Travel to a different time with two powerful
and engaging stories of romance, adventure
and faith every month.

Love Inspired® Suspense:
Enjoy four contemporary tales of intrigue
and romance every month.

Steeple
Hill®

*Available every month wherever books are
sold, including most bookstores, supermarkets,
drugstores and discount stores.*

TITLES AVAILABLE NEXT MONTH
Available June 30, 2009

SECOND CHANCE FAMILY by Margaret Daley
Fostered by Love

Whitney Maxwell is about to get a lesson in trust—and family—from an unexpected source: her student Jason. As she and his single dad, Dr. Shane McCoy, try to help Jason deal with his autism, she realizes her dream of a forever family is right in front of her.

HEALING THE BOSS'S HEART by Valerie Hansen
After the Storm

When a tornado strikes her small Kansas town, single mom Maya Logan sees an unexpected side of her boss. Greg Garrison's tender care for her family and an orphaned boy make her wonder if he's hiding a family man beneath his gruff exterior.

LONE STAR CINDERELLA by Debra Clopton

The town matchmakers have cowboy Seth Turner in mind for history teacher Melody Chandler, but all he seems to want to do is stop her from researching his family history. Seth's afraid of what she'll find, especially when he realizes it's a place in his heart.

BLUEGRASS BLESSINGS by Allie Pleiter
Kentucky Corners

Cameron Rollings may be a jaded city boy, but God led him to Kentucky for a reason, and baker Dinah Hopkins plans to help him count his bluegrass blessings.

HOMETOWN COURTSHIP by Diann Hunt

Brad Sharp fully expects his latest community service volunteer, Callie Easton, to slack off on their Make-a-Home project. But her golden heart and willingness to work makes Brad take a second look, one that could last forever.

RETURN TO LOVE by Betsy St. Amant

Penguin keeper Gracie Broussard needs to find a new home for her beloved birds. If only Carter Alexander, the man who broke her heart years ago, wasn't the only one who could help. Carter promises that he's changed, and he's determined to show Gracie that love is a place you can always return to.